Perry S. Heath

A Hoosier in Russia

The only white tsar. His imperialism, country and people

Perry S. Heath

A Hoosier in Russia
The only white tsar. His imperialism, country and people

ISBN/EAN: 9783337298746

Printed in Europe, USA, Canada, Australia, Japan

Cover: Foto ©Andreas Hilbeck / pixelio.de

More available books at **www.hansebooks.com**

A HOOSIER IN RUSSIA.

THE ONLY WHITE TSAR—HIS IMPERIALISM, COUNTRY AND PEOPLE.

By Perry S. Heath.

FULLY ILLUSTRATED.

THE LORBORN PUBLISHING COMPANY.
NEW YORK, BALTIMORE, CHICAGO.

1888.

CONTENTS.

CHAPTER XXII.

CHAPTER XXIII.

CHAPTER XXIV.

A HOOSIER IN RUSSIA.

CHAPTER I.

An American will never forget the strange sensation which possesses him as he crosses the frontier and enters Russia.

There is something in the very atmosphere telling him he has reached the border-line of the realms of the Tsar the moment he approaches it. Unlike any other portion of Continental Europe, a cordon of gendarmes, mounted Cossacks and cavalrymen guard the entrance to Russia, and exclude all who do not pass the scrutiny of the diplomatic and customs officers, as certainly as though the country were enclosed by a stone-wall mountain high.

As the train from Vienna, Berlin, or any of the other cities contiguous to the Tsar's domain, approaches the frontier the passengers are seized with a nervousness amounting to little less than fear.

They have their passports in hand, and families huddle together like flocks of frightened lambs. Frequently a father or mother, brother or sister, in alighting from the train shows traces of anxiety that are painful. Especially are the English and German people possessed of unusual trepidation. The reason is manifest: there is more than a possibility that they may be taken into custody by the officers and hurried away from each other, never to meet again.

The moment the train stops a buzz of voices is heard; a rattle of spurs and a din of sabers clinking. A swarm of officers flock about the carriages. The doors to each compartment are hastily opened, and harsh voices scream in various languages—

"Frontier!"

The minor officials are dressed in light gray suits, with dark, heavy braid. Those next in rank have white canvas coats, and instead of dark canvas caps those of a little larger pattern and white material. The gendarme in command is decked in pure white. On his shoulders are great epaulets, with an abundance of gold braid.

There is an alarming display of side-arms. They begin with sabers of extraordinary length, and so hitched on the belts that every time a step is made the end of the scabbard strikes the floor and keeps tip-tap time with the tread of the wearer. In the belt is a powerful holster and cartridge-box, and oftentimes a dagger. All wear high-top boots, into which are tucked their pantaloon-legs. The officers run at their work with stentorian exclamations.

The flinging open of carriage-doors is immediately followed by the gendarme in command, who snatches the passports from the passengers, and frightens them, especially if they be timid men or inexperienced women, beyond measure. I have seen women thrown almost into hysterics upon crossing the frontier because of the excitement.

On the heels of the military or police officers come the custom-house lackeys. Without a word they rush into the compartment, and jerking the passengers' parcels from the racks, command every one to alight and enter the official quarters, which are little less than an outpost house of detention.

The fastest trains entering Russia are detained at least two hours on the frontier for the examination of passports and baggage; yet the officers go about their work as though there were but fifteen minutes within which to do it.

All of the railway stations are similar in general and external arrangement. They were built on the same architectural designs. They are wooden structures, about sixty feet wide and from one hundred and fifty to three hundred feet in length. All are one-story high, and along the side next the track runs a platform which is frequently covered with planking.

The atmosphere of the general arrangements in the customs officers' rooms is not different from that found on other frontiers, but the procedure of the officers bears no resemblance to that elsewhere. There is no consideration for the passenger's sensibilities. The moment he enters the large room where the baggage is examined, he is told to stand there ; and the language employed in delivering this command is neither mild nor courteous. Sometimes he waits but ten minutes before he sees his luggage thrown on the great counter, and is asked to produce the keys, that the officer may make examination. But it may be that he will stand two hours without the least knowledge of when his irksome wait will end.

Having passed through a score or more custom-houses in other countries during the last two months, I offered, as usual, to assist the officer in his examination of my effects ; but the instant I put my hands in the satchels to empty them and display my possessions the officer placed the palm of his good right hand against my breast and pushed me back. It was a hint that he was capable of performing the official act without help or suggestion. I had heard of the difficulty of entering Russia before I left Vienna, and sent my trunks from that city to be stored in Paris, as I wanted as little baggage for inspection on the Russian frontier as possible.

The officer hastily pulled from the satchels pantaloons, and turning the pockets inside out, and in one or two instances the legs, dropped them on the floor. He squeezed envelopes, in which there was nothing but private correspondence, into crumpled masses ; and socks which were turned one over the other were torn asunder and dropped on the counter or floor. Scarfs were pressed and opened with the closest scrutiny, for the purpose of seeing if there were any valuables secreted therein. A pair of slippers were hammered over the counter, and the greatest possible attention was given two or three memorandum books and novels. The latter were finally sent to the gendarme, who had packed away from the station to his private quarters as soon as he had secured the passports of the passengers.

After an investigation which appeared to be far more searching than was absolutely necessary, the officer, without saying a word, looked at me, threw up his hands, shrugged his shoulders, and walked away, indicating that he had finished his work, and that I could pick up the effects and repack them. An hour later the officer returned with the books he had taken from me.

There is a very stringent high-tariff protective law in Russia which almost excludes the products of other countries; but it was not for the purpose of ascertaining whether I had dutiable goods that there was all this extraordinary and superserviceable display. The laws against the dissemination of literature in Russia in opposition to its form of government must be enforced at all hazards; and this was the primary object of the officers.

The train on which I first entered Russia was not loaded with many passengers, and the examination of baggage, passports, etc., was concluded within a half hour; but we were not permitted to emerge from the station under four hours.

After I had repacked my satchels I carried them into an adjoining room, where were congregated in a buffet the most motley crowd I had ever seen. Elbowing each other about the lunch-counters, with glasses of steaming *chic* (Russian tea) in their hands, and munching great meat muffets, were Turks, Germans, Norwegians, Jews, Russians, Austrians, Frenchmen, Greeks, Persians, Slavs, and representatives of almost every nationality except the American and the English. The American is a prime favorite in the country of the Tsar, but the Englishman is ostracized and despised.

Instantly as I entered the buffet two great, powerful Jews approached me. They were money-lenders, and in every feature resembled the creatures our Saviour turned out of the temple at Jerusalem. One was probably eighty years old; the other sixty. The first stood six and a-half feet in height; he had an enormously large head, the top of which was destitute of hirsute covering, and a full white beard quite two feet in length. His beak—it was not a nose—would have measured five inches, and the hump rivaled that on the camel's back; his ears were as large as my hand. His companion was almost his exact counterpart, except that he was twenty years younger, and his beard was black.

These two men were attired in suits which were a fair compromise between the costume of the Russians and that of the Jews; they wore long ulsters. In their hands they had great rolls of paper roubles. They were linguists, and after addressing me in four or five languages finally struck the English tongue. They solicited an exchange of money, for which they first asked five per cent. discount, and finally dropped to one per cent. They were good samples of the population which has flooded certain portions of Russia from the Holy Land. The Jews are a despised race in Russia, because their wits have made them rich and the people they have preyed upon extremely poor.

After some time in
this room I picked up
my luggage and start-
ed to emerge. At the
door three or four
gendarmes presented
themselves and com-
manded me to remain where I was.
It was a dreary hour that I spent
there. Finally there was a great
clatter on the outside; a new din
of spurs and swords, and another
army of officers. The commandant
had returned with the passports,
which are too sacred to be intrusted
to a subordinate. Now the doors were opened and the passengers
were permitted to re-enter the carriages and prepare for a continua-
tion of their railway journey.

When we had taken our seats and readjusted our luggage, the officer in charge re-entered our compartment, and to my great surprise

recognized every one from whom he had taken a passport, and, without error, handed back to each his papers.

Fortunately I had taken the precaution before leaving Washington to have my passport *viséd* by the Russian minister, which saved me the trouble of applying for the countersign of an American minister or consul abroad. The best endorsement an American can secure on his passport in embarking for a trip to Russia is the signature of the Russian minister to the United States—if he can get it.

There were others on the train who were not so fortunate as I.

A couple of ladies and four or five men were detained. Two of the men, I subsequently learned, were suspected of having designs on the government, while the others had not procured the proper *vise* on their passports.

One of the men detained was an Englishman, who had shown some officiousness in the customs officers' room during the inspect'on of his baggage. He was from London, and carried with him t vo great leather trunks, which were dumped into the cage—a large compartment surrounded by wire or lattice-work, in which technical examinations of baggage are made—and he insisted upon following them. The officer pushed him back and demanded his keys. The Englishman produced them, and opened the trunks, in which was evidently nothing of objectionable character; but when the man saw his effects poured out on the floor he protested, and his objections caused him a detention from which I have often wondered how he extricated himself.

A wise man never complains at the acts of a Russian officer. To complain leads to detention ; for the Russian officers are as suspicious as they are officious, and all stand in together and have such unlimited license that the stranger is completely at their mercy. If you want to growl, keep your mutterings to yourself and swear when you get back.

A more complete black-list system could not be prepared than is found here. Every year the government issues a book for the use of its officers, in which are given the names of all persons, as far as can be obtained, from all parts of the world, who have ever by word or deed antagonized the Russian government or its forms or institutions. The first thing the officer does when he gets possession of the passport is to examine the black list and see if the name is recorded. If it is not, he then scrutinizes the form of the passport ; and if it is found correct and the *vise* is proper, the duties of that officer end and those of the customs officer begin. Should the effects of the traveler be found passable by the customs officer, there is then no objection to an entrance into the country.

Many of the passengers were deprived of reading matter. It is very unwise for a traveler to take with him into the Tsar's country any works of sentiment. If a book is found in his possession or a letter is discovered on his person, in which there is any criticism of Russian institutions or comment made upon the laws or manners of the empire, or a constitutional form of government is suggested, the possessor is instantly suspected, detained, and possibly sent in exile to Siberia.

Many of the Russian officers neither read nor speak English; and if the color of the cover of a book or an illustration strikes them as unusual the volume is confiscated.

I learned at the frontier that it was not safe to make a memorandum of my travels, and trusted everything to memory, so far as the expression of facts or feelings was concerned.

It was early in the morning when the frontier was reached, and almost noon when the station agent ran out of his office with a dinner bell in hand and began rushing up and down the long platform, ringing and yelling like mad, "Aboard!"

After this exciting exercise had progressed a full minute, the engineer of the locomotive screamed out on the escape-pipe, the fireman pulled the bell, the guardsmen blew their whistles; there was a response from the baggageman; the conductor, rigged like a Napoleon, emerged from the station, and having heard the various signals, cautiously drew from his pocket a long metallic whistle and gave it two or three fierce blows. The train was now ready to start; but it waited some seconds. There was a slight tinkle of the station agent's bell, a toot from the locomotive, little whistles from the guardsmen, a response from the baggage-car, and the corpulent conductor again drew forth his whistle and gave a shrill blast.

Now the locomotive snorted and the train started. The agony was over—I was in Russia.

Four hours in a dull, uninteresting border town had not particularly impressed me.

CHAPTER II

There is no monotony in traveling through Russia. The character of the people and the conveyances offer variety enough for any one.

As the train pulled away from Wierzbolow, the frontier inspection-place, not only were the strangers to Russia thrilled with the surroundings, but also the natives. There were congratulations on every hand over the happy escape from the officials whose officiousness and disregard for persons nearly always ruffle one's feelings. The face of this portion of Russia is similar to that of Wisconsin, less the lakes and beautiful streams; Northern Michigan, without her largest pine trees ; and New Mexico. with the absence of warmth.

The pineries are stunted, the fields covered with wheat—in harvest during August or September—and the villages are of small wooden buildings, covered with straw. Nowhere is there architecture, taste or cleanliness displayed ; while everywhere may be seen barbarians, traces of ignorance and downright brutality. The advancement of the country may be illustrated in the statement that, though Russia is one of the greatest in wheat producing, the cereal is sown broadcast, harvested with the sickle, threshed with the flail, and three-fourths of the work is done by women. The forests are infested with wolves and other wild animals; the fields, when not carpeted with wheat, are covered with Jean-Marie, with a yellow rattle and a plume of blue leaves at the top. Mushrooms and all the fungi of a cold climate are seen ; and one's bewilderment increases as the slow train goes further and further into the empire.

It was the first of August when I passed over this scope of country, and the scenery, though primitive and in many respects familiar, when compared to that of portions of the United States, was deliciously refreshing and interesting. As the train rolled on from the frontier toward Warsaw, the Capital of Poland—now ruled by Russia—and to St. Petersburg, the Capital of Russia, I could not drive from my mind the proverb : "The gates of Russia are wide to those who enter, but narrow to those who would go out."

The Poles are, in general character, like the Germans ; but they are in some respects more enterprising. Their cities have many modern improvements, and in their factories and shops are found traces of the American inventive genius in the way of labor-saving machinery. Some of the older cities in Poland, and especially some of the little old towns, are quaint beyond description.

There have been no improvements made in the railroads of Russia, although their construction was begun more than a quarter of a century ago. They were built under contract for the government by Winans, a Baltimorean, who preferred railroad construction to participation in the American civil war. The parent lines were constructed in the form of a triangle from Warsaw to St. Petersburg ; thence to Moscow, and back to the Capital of Poland. There was a dispute among the civil engineers who were designated to survey the route of the road ; some of them insisting that the line should worm around in its course, so as to reach all of the cities and villages, which would make it circuitous.

Finally there was a dead lock, and the officers went to the Tsar for arbitrament. The Tsar was greatly perplexed over the situation. He saw the necessity of making the railroad lines traverse the thickly-populated sections of country and of reaching the trade marts. In the frenzy of the situation Alexander took a straight-edge rule, laid it down on the map, and drew a direct line from terminus to terminus, without any regard whatever to the face of the country, the population or the trade centers. The Emperor had decided, and his mandate was obeyed.

This accounts for the absence of cities and villages along the railroad lines through old and well-improved portions of the country. Sometimes the traveler sees from the carriage dozens of little cities and hamlets before the train stops at one of them. Those in the distance range from one to ten miles from the track, and are old places. They were simply left out of consideration in the arbitrary determination of the route of the railroad, and the improvements were too valuable to warrant the impecunious population in moving up to the line.

The Russian passenger carriages are a compromise between those in America and those in England as to length, and between France or Switzerland as regards arrangement. They are longer by one compartment than the European carriages, yet internally are identical.

But one *wagon lit*—sleeping car—is run between Vienna or Berlin and Warsaw. At the latter place international communication is cut off, the German and Austrian railroad companies not being permitted to run sleeping-cars or passenger coaches into the Russian Empire. There is nothing like international amity or comity with Russia. Everything must be Russian and for Russia.

There are the first, second and third-class passenger carriages, the same as are found in other portions of Europe, and the consequent

A RUSSIAN VILLAGE—EXCHANGE OF COMMODITIES.

variations in rates of transportation. The speed is much less than in any other civilized country through which I have traveled. The locomotives are the old-fashioned wood-burners. They are fed with cotton-wood, or white pine; and as they have a spark and cinder-arrester, do not trouble the passenger with smoke or any disagreeable particles.

Twenty miles an hour is an excellent average for the express trains, of which class there is only one each way every twenty-four hours. A freight train follows with passenger accommodations. This makes an average of about ten miles an hour. It requires sixty hours to run from Vienna or Berlin to St. Petersburg. The distance would be covered in the United States within forty hours.

It is probably fortunate for the traveler that there are so few stations where the trains can stop, as from three to fifteen minutes are given at every village or city. Directly the train comes to a halt the guardsmen rush along, and opening the doors of the compartments cry out the time which the train will remain. There seems to be a conspiracy between the restaurant-keepers and the railroad officials, for no sooner do the doors open to the compartments than vendors of *chic*, and all kinds of drinkables and eatables, flock about and make a display. Natives usually jump out of the train and into the buffet. An ordinary Russian can drink a glass of tea every time a train stops, should he travel continually. The tea in Russia is probably the finest in the world. It is brought directly overland from China and Japan, and the natives claim that it retains all of its natural fragrance and flavor by not being subjected to ocean travel, which they insist ruins the tea taken to America. It is made in a samovar—a brass or copper tea steamer, heated by the burning of charcoal in a cylinder through its center, or by an alcohol lamp at its base.

Russian tea is always served in glass. It should have a squeeze of lemon and a lump of cut-loaf sugar. There is a richness about it, it must be admitted, which cannot be found elsewhere. It is usually of a deep yellow hue and has a positive body to it.

The best feature of the railroads throughout the empire is the ballast. The iron has been well laid, the grades moderately proportioned, and there is an atmosphere of security when one looks at the road-bed ; but the instant he moves off in a train his delusion vanishes. The locomotive groans, belches out a load of sparks and ashes ; the carriage reels like a drunken man, and as if it would leave the rails ; and you unconsciously cling to whatever there may be stationary in your compartment. I shall never forget my introduction to the Russian way of travel by rail.

At every station a force of men with hammers pound all the wheels on the cars and carriages, to see that they are sound. The pounding has due respect to time and is rather musical. These men are necessary during the winter, when the air is so cold that all metal is endangered ; and I presume they keep up their work in the summer as much to maintain discipline as anything else. The high tariffs and the growth of business enabled the railroad companies to make many improvements last year in the way of station-houses and homes for employes. I do not remember to have seen an elevator or grain warehouse, although this is such a great wheat-producing country.

It was six o'clock in the morning when I arrived from Vienna at Warsaw, some distance within the territory of the Tsar. Warsaw impresses the stranger somewhat in the proportions of Wilmington, Del., or Wilmington, N. C., yet it has ten times the population. The streets are broad and roughly bouldered; the buildings, of brick, stone and wood, are dingy, and the signs of the commercial houses are gaudy and numerous.

When I arrived at the depot on the south of the city, with bundles in hands, I hastened to find a drosky to transfer me to the station on the north side, and three miles distant. Here, as in Berlin and other portions of Germany, the check system for conveyances at the railway stations is in practice. As I made my way to the point of egress, an officer of the railroad handed me a check, and when I got outside of the building I held this up to the view of the army of drivers seated on their vehicles in front of the station. The driver whose number I had came to me at once, took my luggage and helped me into his drosky—a long, slender, open, one-horse phaeton, with wheels eighteen inches in diameter in front and two feet in the rear, with a low seat in the fore and a higher one aft, and with no protection or rest at the sides or back. The driver hustled about in the most excited manner, impressing me with the idea that we had just enough time to reach our destination. To the inquiry he fired at me in the unintelligible tongue, I simply held out my railroad book, pointed to "St. Petersburg," and shrugged my shoulders. He knew I was bound for the Capital of Russia, and soon we were flying through the main thoroughfare of Warsaw, the drosky bounding over the rough stones so like mad that I could scarcely keep my seat by the aid of a firm grip with either hand.

I did not converse with my driver, who whistled softly to his long-bodied and glossy animal, that the speed might be augmented at every jump. Little stretches of Nicholson-block streets were passed, when the wheels of the drosky gave a sound like the rumbling on a bridge, and the sharp rattle and clang of the wheels and hoofs continued on the harsh stones.

There was little vegetation in the city, no smoke or roar from factories, no cheerful faces and merry laughter; all was stern, harsh and foreign. People were gathered in front of the churches on

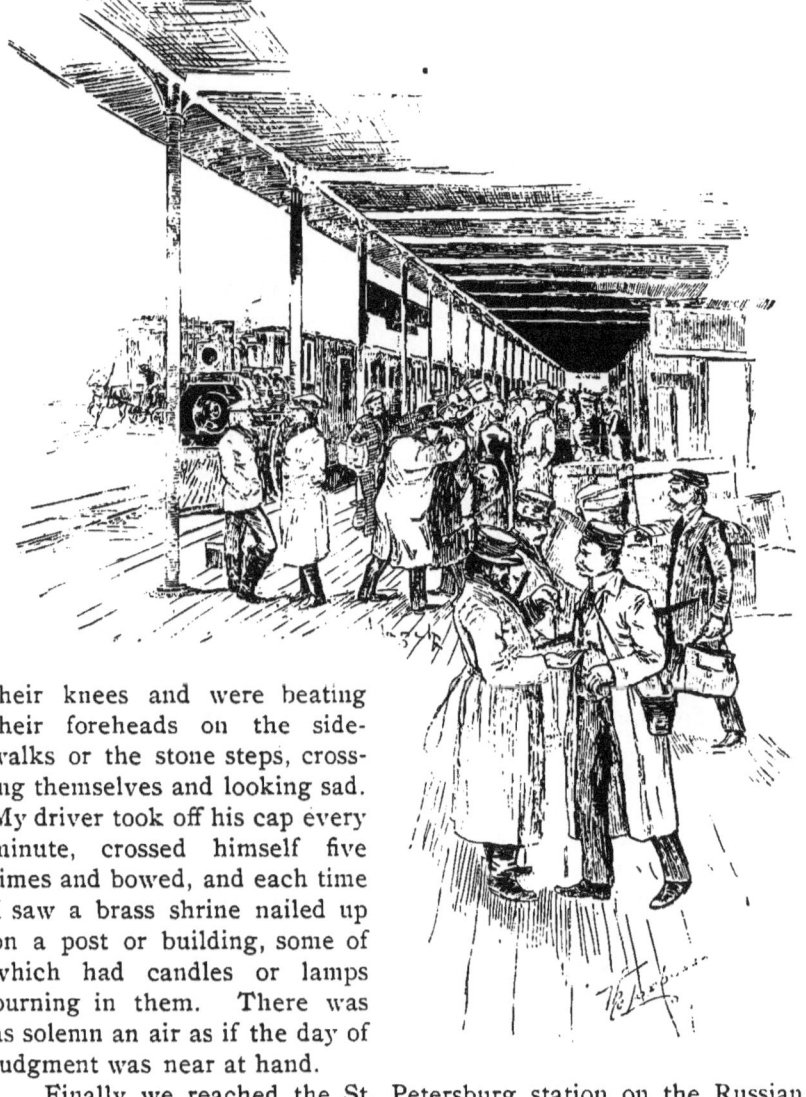

their knees and were beating
their foreheads on the sidewalks or the stone steps, crossing themselves and looking sad.
My driver took off his cap every
minute, crossed himself five
times and bowed, and each time
I saw a brass shrine nailed up
on a post or building, some of
which had candles or lamps
burning in them. There was
as solemn an air as if the day of
judgment was near at hand.

Finally we reached the St. Petersburg station on the Russian
railroad. It was a brick building, one story, hundreds of feet in
length. On one full side was an open corridor or covered platform.
I was met by a half-uniformed officer, who took charge of my bundles

(for a half rouble), and after giving my driver three roubles, I was ushered into a waiting-room, where were seated people from every country on the globe, except North America.

Here I encountered more money-changers. They were mostly Jews—tall, fierce-looking, shrewd fellows, with handfuls of paper roubles and metallic copeck-pieces. The rouble was originally intended to be worth a dollar in American money, but is now worth but forty-six cents. The copeck is the unit of value. One hundred copecks make a rouble.

It took me but a short time to learn that there was no one in the vast station who could speak English, as I employed the waiter in the restaurant to ascertain. There were the customary gendarmes on every hand, strutting around in gorgeous uniforms, with rattling swords, spurs and pounds of epaulets and gold braid, eyeing me in a painful way. The train for St. Petersburg, I soon learned by the use of poor French, stood ready for departure. It was the "Fast Express," composed of probably fifteen old carriages, freight cars and first-class coaches. I had been told all through Switzerland, France, Austria and Germany that I would find the comfortable things of travel in Russia ; and here they were to begin.

It was not yet seven o'clock, although the sun was one-third its way across the horizon. I had had no breakfast, and did not know whether I had time to order it, as the efforts I had made to ascertain "when the seven o'clock train would go" had in reality proven futile. So I went from man to man, with watch in hand, pointing to the train and then to the dial, intimating, by grunts and gestures, that I desired to know when my journey began. All shook their heads and eyed me suspiciously. Even the ticket-seller shook his head.

It then dawned upon me that the train's departure depended upon orders or business from another point, and I sat down at a table to await a broiled chop and a cup of tea, with my luggage, which I could not deposit in the train, beside me, so I could make a dash for liberty in the event there should be a movement on the rail. Meanwhile I braced up from the night of wear with a draught of vermouth. It was after eight o'clock when the last of my breakfast disappeared. And yet the train—the seven o'clock train—moved not.

I employed another man to assist me in either finding when the cars would start or a man who could speak English. Together we labored zealously for two hours, every second appearing to be the one when the train would leave. It was not a pleasant suspense, in view of the fact that Warsaw has a Governor-General, who inspects passports independently of the frontier officers, and as mine had not there been called for I did not know but that I should be detained as I was on the point of departure.

As I paced up and down the platform and through the various rooms of the station I discovered that I was the main object of attraction for two or three hundred people. I could hear the words "German," "English," "American," from the lips of the gendarmes as I passed them in groups. Finally, a man ran from the ticket-room and began ringing a bell. The locomotive responded by a whistle. The trainmen were all excitement, and were rushing to and fro, crying something which even a native could scarcely distinguish; and then I was caught by the arm and pushed inside a room.

It was a gendarme who did it. But he was good-natured about it, and simply motioned the direction I must take to get out of the place and to the train. This procedure made it necessary for me to show my ticket, that no mistake should be made in reference to taking the proper train. There was, however, but one train. When I re-emerged on the platform and started to my compartment I discovered why I was the object of so much curiosity. I wore the only linen ulster in sight, and the only traveling cap in the crowd. It was not on account of not being marked by the passport officer, and I was not molested.

The train made fifteen miles an hour. It swung from side to side as if it would be derailed. Involuntarily I clutched the window-facing and the seats. I was alone in the compartment, and the doors on either hand were fastened from the outside. The carriages on this train were similar to those in other parts of the Continent, composed each of four distinct compartments, in which eight persons may sit; and passengers are never visited by trainmen till they reach their destination, when their tickets are asked for. The train scarcely moved as it passed over the little bridges.

At the first station, an hour distant from Warsaw, there was a sudden stop. The trainman for my section jerked open the door to my right and in Russian, then in German, announced that the trai , stopped ten minutes.

I alighted.

A crowd of people from the country roundabout were in to see *le chemin de fer*—the steam cars! I presume the stop was made largely for the purpose of gratifying the curiosity of the people, as no business was transacted.

When the time for departure came the station-master tapped a large brass bell; the man in the baggage-car blew a police whistle; the conductor answered in the same tone; the engineer touched the locomotive whistle, and then the train moved. At every station the stop was from three to fifteen minutes, business or no business, and this same rigamarole system of signals was each time scrupulously enforced. The train's guard explained that it was to give the passengers time to eat that so many stops were made.

At every station, as on the border of the frontier, there was a restaurant, owned by the railroad's management, and women and children rushed about disposing of pastry, wines, beer and the all-popular *chic*.

There is one advantage to the infrequency of villages along the railroad, where trains stop, and which the traveler enjoys: he is taken from and to the principal cities by the most direct line. There are but half-a-dozen or less railroads in all of Russia, which is about 16,000 miles in length, and these few roads are short and bad. The longest stretches of road are from Warsaw to St. Petersburg, thirty-six hours; from there to Moscow, fourteen hours; and from Moscow to Niijni Novgorod, and then to Warsaw.

Sleds used to run between St. Petersburg and Moscow in twenty-four hours. Now the trains—two a day—occupy more than half that time in making the distance. In America it would require but six hours. The cost of travel is twenty-five per cent. higher than in the United States.

In a travel of many thousand miles in Russia I have never seen a house or shed for the protection of rolling-stock. The locomotives, when not in use, stand exposed on the side-tracks till they rust and fall to pieces. There is the most dense ignorance among the employes about the running of trains. But two of the principal trains in the country have sleeping-cars, and these are patronized only by the strangers. At that time—1887—Russia was attempting to negotiate a loan for the purpose of constructing a line which would connect all of her vast empire, and which was intended to be the greatest railroad enterprise in the world.

CHAPTER III.

Late in the evening of the next day I arrived at St. Petersburg, the Capital of and the most beautiful city in Russia.

Three days and two nights of constant travel, ever encountering perplexities, and through one night compelled to sit up in my compartment, alone in a strange and almost barbaric country, did not prepare me to appreciate the splendor of the surroundings as I crawled out and stood upon the *terra firma* of the parent empire.

Peter the Great selected the site on which St. Petersburg now stands. The old Capital is Moscow, whence the Emperor, about a century ago, removed the imperial scepter here. It is strange the reverence Russians bear toward their ruler; yet the natives of the land of the Tsar speak with the utmost irreverence of Peter the Great. He had many of the traits of the autocrat which have made the name of the Tsar a terror to the world. He was not always humane, but he had that faculty for discernment which, had it been transmitted to his successors, would have made Russia to-day far more civilized than she is. Peter the Great was the lineal heir to the throne. He was a prince by birth. Yet he had the instinct of the statesman.

He saw an opportunity for building up the material interests of the land over which he was to rule; and in order that he might begin at the beginning, he left his country, proceeded to Holland, and learned the trade of a ship-builder, starting at the lowest round of the ladder and rising to the topmost position in the trade. This gave him an insight into the building of navies, which aided him so materially in establishing Russia's maritime power.

Immediately upon his ascension to the throne of the Russias he expressed a desire to live in a palace from which he could view the surrounding country. He wanted to live near the sea, with whose grandeur he was greatly impressed, and to have a place where he could look out upon the enemy, should he approach by land or water.

With this in view he established St. Petersburg, which is popularly known as the Tsar's Window.

Nearly all of the modern architecture in Russia is found in the Capital. Moscow, which has quite as many people, but which covers less ground, is so old that its ancient structures mar the beauty of the new ones. The most improved plans were contemplated and employed when St. Petersburg was surveyed, and the Government extended assistance in making the buildings and the thoroughfares as handsome as possible.

Situated at a somewhat higher elevation than the surrounding country, St. Petersburg is, indeed, the Tsar's Window. From her streets one can, with the naked eye on a clear day, see Finland, beyond the Gulf of Finland, immediately to the south. The shore lines in the distance appear like the battlements of a fortress, and the smoke from her cities and factories can be definitely discerned.

Away to the east the eye realizes the outlines of Peterhof, the island on which are located the royal palaces of the Tsar and his family—an island scarcely a mile square, covered with native forests and cultivated groves; and dotted with fountains and lakes, and the most splendid buildings in the world. No one is permitted to live on this island except he be connected with the Tsar's family.

Up the beautiful little river Neva, to the west, the eye perceives bluffs which rise almost to the dignity of mountains, and which are heavily wooded, dotted with factories and the homes of the suburban inhabitants. The Fortress is located up the river, on a miniature island; and being the dreaded place of detention for Nihilists and suspected conspirators against the Government, no one who knows its awful meaning ever looks toward it or speaks its name except with a shudder.

The streets of St. Petersburg are broad, level, and paved with boulders, Nicholson blocks of wood, or granite. The most substantial buildings are constructed of a light-colored brick. Those occupied by the Government are painted a uniform color of light yellow; and always in front of the places where the military is stationed are posts painted white and black.

The streets of the city are ever thronged with natives and visitors; and it would be difficult to find in any portion of the globe a more cosmopolitan people than one encounters upon the streets here.

There is a predominance of Germans after the natives; and then in proportion are Swedes, Norwegians and French. Turks, Slavs,

Jews and Cossacks are regarded a part of the natives, and are never referred to as foreigners, except by the natives, who turn upon them at times in fiery passion. The Cossacks, as a whole, are highly regarded by Russians. They were the aborigines of Russia; and not only fought her early wars and brought to her the laurels she won on the field in the last two centuries, but they stand foremost to-day among her soldiery.

PETERHOF PALACE AND FOUNTAIN.

At the time I visited St. Petersburg there was but one really good hotel; and there is everywhere in the kingdom an entire absence of hawkers about the railroad stations. Criers for hotels, conveyances and bazaars, and every conceivable trade establishment, are never found in Russia.

The moment the traveler alights from the train in the great station at St. Petersburg he is directed by a railway official to the inside gate, whence he emerges to the public space, which is like a great courtyard on the outside. Here the gendarme in charge of the drosky-stand is encountered. The system of handing numbered checks to arrivals, so that conveyances may be engaged in turn, thus avoiding confusion, and which prevails in Warsaw, is practiced throughout Russia. You take your check, like that for a piece of baggage, and after a few steps find yourself before a large body of drosky and carriage drivers. They wear long robes of navy blue cloth, almost touching the ground. Around their waists are heavy bands of the same material. On their heads are perched low but broad-top caps, with a short rim. All have their pantaloons tucked into the high tops of their boots. The boot-legs have the regulation wrinkles in their center, made with a precision that is artistic. The traveler, if he speaks Russian, calls out his number, and instantly the driver to whom the number belongs doffs his cap and runs forward in the most humble manner; steps up to you; bows, takes your luggage, and directs you to his conveyance.

The finest horses to be found in the world can be seen in St. Petersburg. They are an improvement of the Arabic breed. If nothing else is scrupulously and conscientiously cared for the horses in St. Petersburg have attention. The majority of them are black, and all have tails so long that they almost touch the ground; and their manes are proportionate. The coats of the animals are glossy, and if the driver discovers a speck of dirt upon his horse he instantly stops, takes off his cap, brushes the dirt away and gives the place where it was a high polish, as a fastidious man would polish his beaver.

There is a law which prohibits the exportation of horses from Russia, and likewise their importation, so that there is never the introduction of foreign blood. The animals are driven at break-neck speed through the crowded streets.

At the hotel the traveler is received with great pomp. When the carriage arrives a flock of porters rush out to relieve the stranger of his luggage, and immediately the proprietor extends a hand of welcome.

At the leading hotels, the ranking banks and other commercial establishments in the large cities, the American encounters at least one and sometimes as many as three men who speak his tongue; but it is necessary to have a guide for shopping or sight-seeing expeditions.

In no country which I ever visited have I experienced as much disappointment as in Russia in the matter of familiarizing myself with the customs of the people. In London, Paris, Rome and through Austria, Switzerland and other countries, I was informed that I would find in Russia any number of people who spoke the English tongue, and that every well-regulated store had linguists. All educated Russians, I was assured, spoke English. The very opposite I found to be true. There are many people in St. Petersburg, Moscow and other Russian cities who speak the vernacular, but they are very few in comparison with those who speak only Russian, French or German. On an average, an English-speaking Russian is found in not more than one business establishment in forty.

All of the principal cities of Europe, as well as most of the small ones, and the villages in fact, are swarming with guides. In St. Petersburg I soon learned that there were not more than two guides for the whole city. One of them had a world-wide reputation, and was frequently engaged three months ahead. Fortune favored me here, and I secured the old guide, and very soon formed the pleasant acquaintance of an aged friend and a high official connected with the Tsar—a gentleman who was for thirty-five years the family physician to Alexander II.

All in the employ of the crown are required to wear a service-badge. It is of silver, in the form of a six-pointed star, and a little larger than a French Napoleon piece. Those in immediate connection with the crown—members of the Privy Council, for instance—wear a service-badge more ornamental than those in inferior positions, and this emblem of office gives *carte blanche* to the bearer and insures for him every privilege that can be acquired in official life. At the markets, in the theatres, passing through the Winter Palace and the private places my official friend was shown more distinction than a Cabinet officer would receive in the United States at the hands of men in the public service.

One scarcely gets settled in his hotel till he is possessed with the spirit of exploring the city. Even in August the atmosphere is bracing, if not chilly, and the great change in scenery the traveler encounters commands him to keep on the constant move.

If there is anything especially cheap, it is the drosky or carriage hire. Two persons ride very comfortably in the drosky, and the expense is but twenty copecks an hour for each passenger. Drawn up against the curb-stone in front of the hotels and public places are seen long lines of droskies, each with the driver asleep on his seat, his head lying in his lap, and the horse in a lapse of content.

A whip is never used. The reins are tied with a large knot, and being two or three feet longer than usual, the end is used for the lash. The driver pulls when he wants greater speed, and slackens up when the animal is to stop. He also makes a sound for faster speed that rumbles under his tongue like the whirr-r-r-r of the partridge.

There are no regulations against fast driving. The occupant of the vehicle is responsible for the damage done; and the driver is willing to go as fast as his employer commands. Before the skill now attained by drivers was achieved, it is stated, the fatal casualties amounted to an average of one person every day in the streets through reckless driving. The driver is not arrested when a foot-passenger is run over. The occupant of the vehicle is taken into custody. This is pleasant for the Russian, but tough for the Yankee.

St. Petersburg is regarded a dull place in summer time. It is the winter that offers all the sports and amusements, and attracts the large crowds. People from all parts of Europe flock here to engage in the sleighing carnivals and holiday festivities, the balls and parties, and theatrical entertainments, which have won celebrity throughout the world.

I found but one place of amusement open, which was the Summer Garden; and here I witnessed extraordinary performances nightly. Sunday is not regarded as a holy day, and many of the factories do not stop on account of it; while work in the streets and on buildings progresses as on week days.

The first night that I attended the Summer Garden I was thrilled with a peculiar sensation. We entered at a wide gate in a high wall, where we purchased and gave up tickets. On the inside was an open park, covering probably two acres. In the center of it was a canopy under which the nobility and aristocracy of the city drank various beverages and partook of luncheon. It was such a scene as one witnesses in some of the highest-class gardens in Berlin and other German cities.

At about ten o'clock, when darkness had come on, the band called the multitude from the Garden into an adjoining open space, for which extra tickets were required. We entered what appeared to be a public square, in which were wooden seats. In front of this was the side of an enormous theater. The glaring lamps from the garden shed a reflective light upon the space we now occupied. Finally the side of the theater seemed to move away. It was a curtain rising; and a large stage was disclosed before us. This was the Summer Theater. Nothing but the canopy of Heaven was over our heads. We sat there in the open air and witnessed a tragedy, a comedy, and an opera, on a stage which occupied the rear of the Winter Theater. It was after midnight when the entertainment closed, and the Summer Garden was patronized until daylight, which breaks in August at half-past two or three o'clock in the morning.

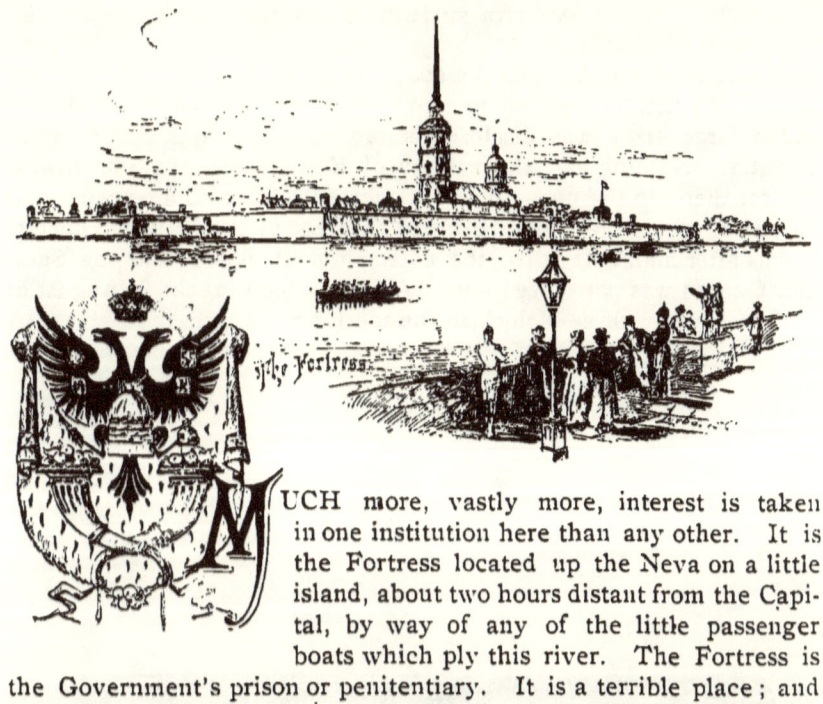

The Fortress

UCH more, vastly more, interest is taken in one institution here than any other. It is the Fortress located up the Neva on a little island, about two hours distant from the Capital, by way of any of the little passenger boats which ply this river. The Fortress is the Government's prison or penitentiary. It is a terrible place; and the natives shudder when they hear it mentioned, or the scenes which are known to be enacted within its dismal walls recur to them.

Few stories are told from the lips of inmates of this horrible prison, as the civilized world seldom hears of the man, woman or child once sent there.

If the Fortress could speak it could tell of more cruelty, injustice and heartlessness than all the pages of Russian history. It is true that Russia is the home of the Nihilist—the original conspirator against monarchical government, imperialism and absolute power vested in the single man. And the American, after a short stay in the empire, does not wonder that there are Nihilists, or that the result is a Fortress and prison where suspects and open enemies of the crown are consigned for life or execution.

Surrounding the Fortress is a broad stone wall on which sentries pace day and night.

At each corner is a parapet, where the superior officers of the guard keep vigil, and are prepared for any effort which may be made by friends of inmates at rescue. None but the officers are permitted to land here. I have heard many stories, most of which I believe to be true, about strangers losing their lives in attempts to stop at the Fortress. While boating they innocently run up to the walls, and in attempting to land have been shot down. The guards have imperative orders to permit no one, except certain authorized officers, to place his foot upon this little island, the outlines of which are marked by the high, grim and death-like walls.

When one is suspected of designs against the present form of government he is instantly arrested and taken to the House of Preventive Detention, where he awaits the form of mock trial. He is given no opportunity to send for witnesses, to employ counsel, or to make the usual defense. He is arraigned by the officers of the crown, who are supposed to stand in the same attitude toward the prisoner that the Judge Advocate occupies in the courts-martial in the United States. He is presumed to give justice to the suspected, and render it to the Government. There is no appeal; when the decision is announced the prisoner is hurried away to the Fortress. After that the world does not know what becomes of him. He is absorbed in the Unknown, like the drops of water in the ocean.

Natives say that if the blood shed in this place was turned into one single stream it would float a ship. The rankest criminals and the most innocent, delicate women are brought face to face here.

The structure itself is after the usual fortress architecture. It was originally constructed for the purpose of defending the approach to St. Petersburg; but the Tsar soon came to the conclusion that the Neva would never be a stream which an enemy would occupy with men-of-war, and that on account of its narrowness it could be held by batteries on the shore. The Fortress was then turned into a prison.

There are no crimes in the country punishable by death, except those against the crown. A man may murder a whole houseful of people in cold blood and escape with a five or one-year sentence, if he does not in fact escape without any punishment; but if he criticises the Government, the Tsar, a member of the royal family, or an officer, he is condemned to be shot, or is exiled for life to Siberia.

The same punishment is meted to the tutors in the schools for advocating a constitutional or other form of government than that which now prevails. It is significant that nearly all of the riotous public demonstrations and attempts against the life of the Tsar on account of imperialism have, for many years, had their inception in the schools. No sooner does a pupil learn to read, and get into his or her possession books suggesting other forms of government and free institutions, than he or she becomes what is commonly termed a Nihilist—a conspirator against the Government.

It is no wonder that there are less than five millions of Russia's one hundred million subjects who can read or write. The only schools in the Russias are those established and maintained at the expense of the crown. Appointments to the schools are made by the royal families who support the Tsar in every effort he makes to tax the population more heavily, or bring down the thumb-screws finally in his strife to strangle education. There are continual changes in the rolls of teachers in the schools; and detectives are among the pupils, or are constantly in some capacity about the buildings. As soon as it is suspected that there is sedition taught or permitted, or that any form of dissatisfaction is finding a lodgment in the pupil's mind, the teacher or the child is instantly removed; and if his ideas are deep-seated, or considered dangerous, he is sent to the House of Preventive Detention for the development of his disease or the punishment of his crime.

The streets of St. Petersburg continually swarm with detectives, dressed as citizens. There are about thirty thousand of them in the Capital alone.

Besides these, there are from twenty-five to seventy-five thousand soldiers constantly stationed here and at Peterhof, about the palaces of the Tsar. Many of the detectives are taken from the ranks of the army. They know every stranger who enters the city, and keep a close surveillance upon him.

The first thing the traveler upon entering a Russian city or village does is to give up his passport to the landlord. Your passport is asked for before your name; and, in fact, before the porter releases his grip upon your luggage. If you have not a passport you must leave the building instantly, as your arrival has already been reported at the headquarters of the gendarmerie the minute you enter the building; and but a short hour is given the landlord within which to send your passport to headquarters. A heavy fine is imposed upon landlords if they fail to turn in passports immediately upon their receipt; and this has the effect of making them extremely cautious. If they are fined several times within a short period they become suspects, are watched as criminals, and are liable to be sent up the river.

It is by this rigid system of prompt action that the detectives are enabled to know every stranger's face when they encounter him on the streets. They follow you into shops, in your drives through the city, and you are never out of their sight.

I was greatly impressed with the rigid guardianship these worthies keep over strangers a few days after my arrival at St. Petersburg. My official friend called one evening, and while talking over Russian matters in my private room in the Hotel d'Europe he forgot his position and joined me in severe criticism of the imperiousness of the crown and the servitude the subjects are placed under. All of the conversation was carried on in very low tones of voice, until some of the every-day occurrences were related, and word-pictures were drawn of the manner in which men, women and children against whom there was only the slightest suspicion of disloyalty were snatched out of their beds at midnight, or taken from their homes, shops or factories while at work and carried to the House of Preventive Detention, given summary forms of trial and hastened to the Fortress, where they disappeared from view forever, without an opportunity to defend themselves or part with their families and friends.

At this point our voices could have been heard by one in an adjoining room or in the corridor outside the door. Quick as a flash my friend threw up his hands, and exclaimed, softly, between his teeth :

"Hist!" and he drew his chair nearer me. "You must speak in a whisper! We may be detected here. There are detectives all about us. They are located in this very hotel. Their ears and eyes may be at our door. If I should be found in your room I would be suspected. If one of your words should be heard by these officers you would be condemned, and no influence I could wield and nothing that your Government could do would save you."

Further admonition was unnecessary.

In the dining-room, on the streets, at the theater, the Summer Garden, the church, one feels that the eyes of detectives are upon him, and that every move he makes and word he utters is noted by the men whose only motive is to misconstrue and misinterpret. The greatest effort is made to distort what natives and strangers say or do, so as to bring them within the jurisdiction of the criminal code.

There is a constant Reign of Terror.

It does not partake of excitement, but quiet trepidation and fear which are as painful. Whenever a party of gentlemen or ladies, whose character is not known to be far above suspicion, enter a public place for amusement or refreshment a stranger in appearance but a detective in fact gets within ear-shot or eye-sight. If anything is said or done which is in the least suspicious, he draws nearer and makes a note. Instantly the party is under the ban of suspicion.

The principal operations of the gendarmes and detectives are performed at night. There are nocturnal visitations at the homes of all who are believed to entertain any design or idea against the Government. The natives usually enjoy absolute immunity from these official visitations during the day. The night visitors are headed by detectives, while the visitations in daylight are by the gendarmes. Sometimes a family suspected of designs against the Government, either through positive work or correspondence with persons outside the empire, are visited a dozen times during a day or night by officers. Every conceivable design is sprung upon them, with a view to taking them unawares and finding some traces of evidence of disloyalty. The visitations during the day are by officers in citizen's clothing; and they go about their work so quietly that the service attracts little attention in the neighborhood. But sometimes the night visitors come in a great squad, and surrounding the house a search follows that makes an absolute sensation. The night searches of this kind, besides being designed to find all traces of conspiracy against the Government, are intended to terrorize the community and drive the inhabitants from any seditious intrigue with which they may be connected.

No family feels secure from surprises of this character and no one can congratulate himself that he is above suspicion. Tsars have put detectives after members of the royal family, and their blood has been shed at the Fortress in punishment of the fancied or real crime of sympathizing with conspirators.

One will wonder how it can be that in spite of all this precaution, and notwithstanding the continued espionage of the Russian police, Nihilism can flourish and crime can grow. An educated Russian has a full development of the bump of cunning; and occasionally one is found who is equal to the detectives.

Some years ago the Prefect of the Police drove to a bank in his drosky to draw the money necessary to pay off his forces. The banker handed him his package, which proved to be in bills of larger denomination than those desired. The Prefect asked that they be changed for bills of smaller denominations. The banker said that he could not accommodate him at that moment, but that he would secure the exchange if the officer would come back later. It was then ten o'clock in the morning, and the Prefect promised to return at three in the afternoon. Promptly at three he drove up, and was informed that he must be mistaken, as he had just received the money, not ten minutes before. Without a moment's delay the official sprang into his carriage and drove to the nearest post. It is the custom in St. Petersburg to post detectives at different points along the main thoroughfares, and these detectives are compelled to keep close watch of every passerby, and besides must note the movements of all their superiors. Driving to the first post the Prefect said to the officer:

"Did you see me drive by here a few minutes ago?"

The reply was in the affirmative. He then asked which direction he took, and the direction was pointed out. Going to the next post he made a similar inquiry of the detective stationed there, and was informed that he had been seen to pass a short time before.

Once more he was informed of the direction he had taken, and this time he discovered that he had turned the corner. Driving a short distance down the street indicated he arrived at the third post, and was there told that he had been seen to drive up and stop at the Hotel d'Europe. He hastened to the hotel and inquired the number of his room. Having learned it, he mounted the stairs and proceeded to the chamber which, it was supposed, he occupied. Bursting open the door he confronted a man who was the exact counterpart of himself.

This individual was in the act of storing away the large sum of money he had just received from the bank, and in twenty minutes would have been outside the reach of the gendarmes. His make-up was so perfect that he deceived every one. His drosky was an exact duplicate of that of the Prefect; his horse matched to a hair, and his servants were identical in every respect to those of the Chief of Police.

The plot would have been brought to a successful termination and the bank would have lost an enormous sum of money but for the promptness of the Prefect. As it was, an enterprising criminal, who proved to be of excellent family, was last heard of in the Fortress on the Neva, and he is probably at present expiating his crime in the mines of Siberia.

CHAPTER V.

There are two personages whose words are law—the Tsar and the Prefect of Police.

Russia never had but one code of laws, and that was prepared by Peter the Great, a century and a half ago. It was originally a very crude composition; indefinite, vague, and possible of any construction. It was nothing in the way of a constitution; so that subsequent rulers had only to take from or add to it *ad libitum*, decreasing or enlarging the one-man power at will.

Laws are made in the shape of ukases, which are similar in form to the proclamations issued from the Executive Mansion or executive departments at Washington. The difference in their character is that the ukases are the creation of laws, the outgrowth of desires of the Tsar; while the proclamations and orders issued from the White House and departments at the Capital of the United States are in fulfillment, or are the outgrowth of laws, the legislative power being vested only in Congress. In Russia there is no legislative power except in the Tsar and his Cabinet. They make the laws, like a Congress, and enforce them. The jurists or judges' of Russia are appointed to serve during their life-time.

There is but one set of courts; so that there is nothing like an appeal, when once a decision is rendered, except it be made to the Tsar; and it is quite as easy for a camel to pass through the eye of a needle as it is for a subject to approach him. There is no such thing as the *habeas corpus*. There never was such a recourse. I have not heard that there is any offense against the crown that is bailable. Prisoners are always held for trial—if they are not sent directly to the Fortress, where only the military laws are exercised, and where the courts-martial sit in judgment—at the House of Preventive Detention, the half-way prison between the Fortress and liberty. It is contended by the authorities that the House of Preventive Detention is as good as liberty on bail to the prisoner, as it is possible for him to there receive counsel and visits from his family. A visit, however, from any one at the House of Preventive Detention is a mockery.

The vagueness of the penal code has a design.

It gives unlimited latitude to the courts, so that, when a direction issues from the Tsar or his Council that the prisoner shall be condemned, the laws are construed to this end, should the prosecution fail to convict under the natural process.

Lawyers are extremely scarce here, and their success in the trial of a cause depends solely upon the degree of their solidity with the authorities. If they are subservient, and truckle to the powers, they are favored. Should they stand upon the merits of a cause and attempt only to exercise their judicial learning, they are practically driven from practice. A Russian lawyer would be a poor excuse in the United States.

There is some probate business ; but it does not amount to much, since the bulk of the property is in the hands of the few.

But the most diabolical feature of the trials, and, in fact, all matters of every public character, is the arbitrary power given officials. Americans can appreciate this most keenly if they will fancy trials for high crimes conducted by the Government only, and no appeal or petition possible ; arbitrary and unlimited construction of law by the court ; and its right to cite laws, without reference to date or priority ; repealing almost any ukase or edict. This makes it absolutely impossible for any one to win a suit without the favor of the court.

Alexander II. was far more popular than his son, now on the throne. Despite his maintenance of all the despotic prerogatives of the Tsar, Alexander II. did many things to please his people. Alexander III. is regarded by the Russians as not only a weak man, but a coward. Although the Winter Palace is the finest in the world, he lives at Peterhof, across the Gulf of Finland. There, amid a dozen palaces, stables costing 2,000,000 roubles a year and containing 850 horses, with a salary of about 6,000,000 roubles a year—altogether over $4,000,000—he lives and does the little business he transacts. He is afraid to go anywhere ; he is literally carried by detectives, bodyguards and soldiers, and is suffering from too much power.

One night I attended the illumination at Peterhof in honor of the Tsarina's birthday. This woman is a sister to the future Queen Consort of England, and has no more compunctions about the burdens of her subjects. The Tsar's palace is situated on a peninsula. The grounds and the buildings occupy almost a mile square. There are the most superb structures, fountains, and miles of the finest parking and drives in the world.

Buildings and fountains, trees, and great crowns, crosses and figures, besides miles of high walls, were covered with vari-colored lamps. There were millions of lights, and it required a regiment of soldiers and hundreds of civilians weeks to put them in place. All was paid for from the public treasury, or rather the Tsar's treasury, repleted by the people.

At a time in the evening when the fountains and lights glistened most, the bands played loudest and the pyrotechnics and cannon from the men-of-war in the gulf glared and roared best, the royal family gave the assembled multitude a rare treat. It showed itself. Seldom it is that the people in Russia see their Emperor, their Tsar, because he suspects them all of designs upon his life.

I was making my way between two of the great blazing walls of colored lights, through one of the drives, when a detachment of Cossacks dashed along, slashing their sabers and driving the people out of the way. In their wake came soldiers on foot, and great detachments of men in citizen's clothing. The latter stationed themselves in front of the lines of the masses. A din of voices; lusty cheering is heard in the distance. It comes nearer, then nearer. More Cossacks, more soldiers, more men in citizen's clothing; and further back we are crowded.

The tier of officious citizens is reinforced in our front, and many linger in the drive-way. Finally the caravan comes in view. More Cossacks, soldiers, citizens. Eight white horses, each one on the left bearing a postillion, are next seen; then the royal equipage, an immense, gold-mounted chariot. The Tsar, a great, burly fellow, with full beard, crown and uniform, is on the left seat in front. The brother, the Crown Prince, the Tsarina and Grand Dukes, etc., make up the load. On every side of the carriage, four deep, are Cossacks, while the drive-way in front and rear is blocked by soldiery, making a perfect shield against violent attacks.

The "citizens" who were so very plentiful and officious were the most experienced detectives and body-guards in the empire. There were thousands of them. It would have been impossible for one to have raised his or her hand against the Tsar or any member of his family.

It is the boast of the Russian authorities that their detectives have eyes in every portion of their heads and bodies. The whole service of protecting the crown and members of the family, and suppressing all thoughts of dissatisfaction with the present form of government, is in full charge of General Gresser. chief of the secret service. The authority of this officer is appalling. He can order into exile or the execution-yard anyone suspected of unlawful or disrespectful acts or intentions. He attends the theaters, and may be said to run all places of amusement. If he is displeased with anything he suppresses it, and there is no redress. His word is law, from which there is no appeal.

There are some commendable acts of General Gresser. He permits no unnecessary exposure to fire, or loss of water, and will not tolerate beggary. There are no beggars in St. Petersburg. Recently Chief Gresser was at the Garden Theater, where the usual performance takes place on the stage, and where people enjoy the refreshments at hand. One of the waiters at a table made an insulting observation to a lady. The matter was reported to Gresser, who on the spot closed the theater and garden and kept them closed for six weeks, although the daily and nightly profits exceeded two thousand roubles. There was no appeal from the verbal order. The license of other officers is quite as great. That of the Cossack is astonishing.

In the streets of St. Petersburg, Moscow, and other cities, the stranger is attracted by squads of murderous-looking mounted soldiers. They are reared and live on horseback, and are expert horsemen. They wear slouch caps, sash coats, with belts ; top boots, great, jingling spurs, broad sabers, and in their holsters are heavy pistols. Swung across their backs are carbines, in Astrakhan or other cases. They carry the ancient battle-ax, attached to a fifteen-foot staff, swinging it from a socket at the foot-rest. All ride rapidly, are swarthy and rough-looking, and remind one more of war and bloodshed than anybody or anything else.

Throughout the history of Russia the reader sees the hand of the Cossack. He was the first and last in battle. When Napoleon, in 1812, after taking Moscow and leaving his shattered army freezing and starving in the dead of winter to struggle back to France, started on his memorable run to Paris, the Cossacks pursued the fleeing forces and made mincemeat of them. While the French soldiers were freezing in a temperature thirty degrees below zero and filling up the Volga and other streams they attempted to ford, the Cossacks with ease flayed the enemy, one Cossack being equal to twenty French soldiers. The Cossack of old won a local renown that is held sacred ; but he has since degenerated.

Now the Cossack is a plunderer. He is furnished a horse, arms and ammunition, and is given rations when in camp, but must forage when on the march, which is nearly always; and he is given no pay. But for a natural pilferer he is given something better than pay. He has complete immunity against punishment for any crime other than disloyalty and wanton murder. The Government makes him a licensed plunderer, and tells him to forage. He becomes a brigand, and no secret is made of it. Peasants and villages are robbed by these soldiers; travelers garroted, and nothing is said or done about it. The Cossack is a privileged character.

And so much like the ideal of the Tsar is the Cossack that he is made the crown's bodyguard. At Peterhof, and wherever the Tsar is, there one finds a regiment or two of Cossacks, riding like mad, committing depredations, and acting the ruffians they are. They are the best living, moving illustration one sees in all of the Russias of the character of the Government and its ruler.

Winter Palace

One of the first places the visitor to the Capital of Russia inquires for is the Winter Palace. This is the finest public building in the world.

Its contents are valuable beyond computation. It has been said that the jewels alone in this rich treasure-house and residence are worth five hundred and fifty million dollars. Surely there are wagon loads of diamonds, rubies, emeralds and other precious stones, besides carloads of solid gold and silver. A dozen rooms are filled with the most precious tableware.

Here are thousands and thousands of the richest, most artistic and valuable paintings to be found in the world. They are

from the brushes of not only the world's old masters, but the modern
artists of the country. Hundreds of paintings are large enough to
cover almost the entire side of spacious rooms. Some of them are
trophies of war, captured from conquered countries in the last century. The building is fully two blocks, or squares, in length, and
quite as wide, covering as much space as four of the large squares in
Washington and several acres in area. It is of brick, stone and
marble, four high stories and a basement.

In front of the main entrance to the Winter Palace is an immense open court, similar to Trafalgar Square in London. It is beautiful, and ornamented with handsome arrangements for lighting by
gas or electricity. In the center is the Alexander Column. The
building at the main entrance is concave in shape. It has a splendid
drive, and is a popular lounging-place for visitors.

The Winter Palace here faces the war office. In this square
also stands the celebrated statue to Cæsar Peter, and on the left are
the ministerial and judicial departments. In the immediate vicinity
are located all the Government buildings; and around about are situated some of the largest, oldest and most imposing churches, whose
great gilded domes and crosses blaze in the sunlight. The scene in
combination is one of splendor, witnessed nowhere else on the globe.

The Palace of the Hermitage is situated just behind the Winter
Palace, and is externally one of the most dazzling buildings in the
Capital. It is a magnificent structure, the original hermits being the
Empress Catherine II., the nymphs, the princesses and the countesses
of her court. The seat of the empire was formerly at the Hermitage.
The building now contains various beautiful vases in malachite,
lapis lazuli, jasper and other stones of great brilliancy and value.

Stored here is a lapis lazuli vase of oval shape which measures
twenty feet in diameter, being the largest vase in the world. Its
value cannot be computed. Some of these objects are the work of
exiles in Siberia, and were brought over from the Ural Mountains and
other sections of the exile kingdom. The floors of the Hermitage
are of elaborately inlaid oak, cedar and mahogany. The works of
art cannot be described. They successfully rival those at the
Louvre, Paris.

Russians are extremely proud of the treasures they have stored
in the palaces here and at Moscow. They evidently never think of
the sacrifice made and the blood spilled to acquire these treasures;
and they never recur to the fact that they in no way relieve their pov-

erty or assist them to bear the burdens they are constantly subjected
to. Russia probably has ten thousand million dollars in her idle
palaces. This vast wealth is in *bric-a-brac*, paintings, ceramics,
precious stones and jewels, purchased with money wrung from the
people by taxation or secured in war.

With not a free public school, the credit of the empire nearly as
low as that of Turkey, and the treasury constantly almost empty,
these bewilderingly beautiful, priceless and precious jewels are simply
displayed, like so many wax flowers, to the gaze of the gaping visitor. I presume it is for the purpose of impressing not only the
strangers, but the natives, with the gorgeousness of their empire and
the high standard of taste set up by their present ruler and those who
have preceded him.

A palace has been constructed for every Emperor or Empress
who has ruled since Russia was civilized, and the consequence is a
great aggregation of the enormously expensive structures. I walked
five hours, with but infrequent and brief pauses, through the Winter
Palace one day and progressed but half way through its three principal floors. One with an eye for the artistic would be absorbed here
five hours a day for five weeks. He would grow weary of the
pottery and chinaware made centuries ago and down through all
periods of time to the present, and of which there are cartloads;
walls and walls, miles of them, of the most perfect paintings and
prints; royal harness, and carriages, in which have ridden Tsars and
Tsarinas, and their families, beginning three centuries ago and coming down to the present, the trappings all decked with the most precious jewels—diamonds, rubies and emeralds being no more here than
Rhinestones in America—the personal effects of the various rulers who
have stood over Russia with a rod of iron and a will of steel—includ-
ing the playthings they had when they were children.

The Winter Palace was the residence of the Emperor and his court
during the winter months. But Alexander III. occupies his palace at
Peterhof, across the gulf to the east, during the entire year. He
refuses to dwell in the Winter Palace, because his father, in 1881,
lived there; and after several unsuccessful attempts were made to
assassinate him in his home, he was finally torn to pieces by a bomb
thrown from the hand of a Nihilist on the street, and here he was
carried to die. Surely the most ambitious could not but be appalled
by the thought of life in such a temple; and Alexander III. is not
an exception; he simply refuses to live here on account of the super-

stition that it is ill-luck to reside in the house where an ancestor has expired.

The Winter Palace was built over a century ago. Very early it was burned, and in 1839 was entirely rebuilt and restored. The exact frontage of the building at the main entrance is 555 feet. The ball-room has an inlaid oak floor, polished like marble ; the door-knobs and facings are studded with precious stones ; also the chandeliers, and frequently on the walls and ceilings gems blaze and scintillate in the light ; the room is about 90 by 300 feet in length. The dining-room has walls of gilt, and although a little smaller, is quite as brilliant as the ball-room. Before Nihilism became so rampant there was a grand supper and ball given every midwinter by the court, to which the army and navy officers, the civil officers and the nobility were invited.

Among the jewels is the great Orloff diamond. It weighs 795 carats and surmounts the Imperial Scepter. The Imperial Crown of all the Russias is adorned with jewels valued at 823,796 roubles, or $400,000. In general appearance it resembles the dome-formed patri-archal miter, and carries on its summit a cross of five splendid dia-monds, supported by a large uncut but highly-polished spinel ruby.

There are eleven great diamonds in the foliated arch, rising from the front and back of the crown supporting the ruby and its cross. On either side of this central arch is a hoop of thirty-eight vast and perfect pearls, imparting to the imperial diadem the miter-like aspect which is to typify the exaltation of the Sovereign into the sphere of the ancient, superseded patriarchate. The dome-spaces on either side of these arches of pearl are filled with leaf-work and ornaments in silver covered with diamonds and lined with purple velvet. There is a band on which the crown is supported, and it surrounds the brow of the Em-peror, carrying with it twenty-eight immense diamonds. The orb is valued at 190,500 roubles, and is surmounted by a large sapphire of a rich but slightly greenish-blue color, with a huge diamond of the finest water and of a form somewhat elongated. I describe this Im-perial Crown so that the reader may have a general idea of the gorgeousness of the many crowns found in all of the royal palaces of the country. One description will give the general appearance of many of these precious heirlooms. The guide-books will give the details of the palaces ; and since I have resolved not to consult guide-books in the compilation of these notes, wearisome detailed descrip-tions are not entered into.

The Hermitage is the royal art gallery, and, as I have intimated, is the successful rival to the Louvre in Paris or the National Gallery in London. It contains about two thousand pictures selected from more than four thousand specimens. The advancement of Russian art is shown in the Hermitage to splendid advantage. Much has been said about the literature of Russia, but I have been unfortunate in not finding much of it. I must say, however, that I have seen a great deal of artistic work which would do credit to Rome, Florence, or any other home of true art.

It is necessary to have a special permit—which is not easily obtained, but which is secured at one of the offices of the Governor-General—in order to visit either the Winter Palace or the Hermitage. You are received at the entrance by the officers in charge and a guide is assigned to you. If there are several persons in your party several guides assist you, not for the purpose of showing more than one could indicate, but to watch you.

In every room there are detectives or gendarmes in citizen's clothing, and their eyes are ever upon you. The guides seldom speak a word : they confine themselves to conducting you from room to room and floor to floor, and indicating with their hands the most desirable things to be seen. No stipulated charge is exacted, but it is the proper thing to hand each one of those who show you any attention at least fifty copecks before you part with him. There is no place in the world where a liberal use of the filthy lucre oils up the machinery to better advantage than in Russia.

As the visitor goes about the city sight-seeing he is impressed with the profusion of persons in the employ of the established Church of Russia, which is the Greek Church. Very many monks are seen everywhere, and one finally wonders where and how they all live.

The average Greek monk is not of a very high order of man. He is fairly educated, but is slothful. He is dressed in a long robe of dark-brown cloth, with a great black head-dress of the same material. From two to five strands of beads, with immense crosses on them, hang from his neck, while in his right hand he generally carries a large string of beads made from bones, with a crucifix of the same material. His hair is from one to three feet in length, and vies with his full beard in trying to cover his body. The monks are attached to the church, all the buildings of which are owned and run by the Government, and live in the attics or basements of the annexes.

Some of the monks have shown great musical talent. The finest vocal music I have heard on the Continent was by a choir of monks here. Their voices were rich, round, full and highly cultivated, and the music flowed in regular waves like echoes from machinery— not a discord, no rasping, but perfect harmony. Others of the monks develop mechanical ingenuity. They all look after funerals and alms gathering. They live quietly, are not widely known and move about like cats with muffled feet.

There is industry on every hand. And the manual labor in the public places is not confined to the male sex. Women work on the streets with the men, shoveling, using the pick-ax, or driving teams ; and they labor every day in the week. Nicholson pavements were being put down. The blocks were of wood, and the foreman had a novel scheme by which to compel all the men to do the same amount of work. When the blocks are put down and covered with sand they must be pounded in evenly. The men worked in squads of ten or twelve. If pounding or picking is to be done the foreman strikes first ; then the second strikes ; then the third, and so on till the last, sledges and picks coming down in such rapid succession that the last has struck by the time the first has raised his implement. Thus perfect time, like clockwork, is kept. The rattling strokes are musical, too.

Laborers receive but one and a-half roubles a day in St. Petersburg for the most wearing work. For ordinary labor but one rouble is paid, while thousands work for six roubles a month. Domestics receive less than two roubles a month. But this is good pay compared to that received by the soldiers in Russia. A private gets four roubles a year, and the commissioned officers from half to two-thirds the amount paid privates in the American army.

URING an hour's stroll through the streets of the Capital or any of the larger Russian cities almost every class of people on the face of the earth is met; but one encounters none more picturesque and interesting than the drosky driver.

This individual is the sole cabman, the popular hackman, and the protector of the stranger. The drosky and carriage are the only conveyances in Russia. There are no such things as omnibuses, hacks, hansoms, etc., found so generally on the Continent and in England.

The drosky driver is the typical Russian. His vehicle is owned by a capitalist, who hires it out, horse and all, for three roubles a day. The driver charges, on the average, fifty copecks an hour, and, therefore, has reasonable possibilities; but there is so much inclement weather, when riding in an open vehicle is not pleasant, that he has a hard time making both ends meet. He backs up in front of a hotel, market, railroad station or other public place, and sleeps till he is called by a customer. When he first awakens you are impressed

with his apparent utter lack of intelligence. His hair is two inches
thick, cut square around, and parted slightly in the middle. Generally it is of a dirty light blonde. His eyes are milky, light and insipid, the complexion sallow, beard short, light, and often thin. As
he straightens up on the narrow, low seat of his drosky he rubs his
eyes, grunts, receives orders obediently, and is at once all energy.
Nobody is more industrious or faithful, and no one more agile.

Most of the drosky drivers were slaves till the emancipation
proclamation of Alexander II. was issued, about 1861, and not one in
a hundred can read his own name. But he remembers locations, and
is familiar with every foot of ground within his radius. I remember the first day I was at St. Petersburg to have handed a driver an
address written in Russian ; it was that of an official.

"What's that you are giving him?" inquired my courier.

I told him.

"Don't ever expect a drosky driver to read anything. That fellow couldn't recognize his own name if it were printed in letters a
foot long. Don't you see," continued the courier, pointing, "that
all the signs are illustrated here, and that there is little of names and
business in letters? Very few people read here."

The drosky driver seldom has a family, and his horse's bed is his
own. It is nearly always a fine, sleek animal, and the whip is never
used, although he drives very hard. The animal is full of vigor, and
is used to fast steps. The only "coaxer" is a knot in the end of the
reins. This the driver brings down upon the horse frequently and
with effect. You have no difficulty in any Russian city in securing a
fast drive.

For a week in St. Petersburg I employed a drosky with a pretty,
glossy black horse, and the usual gait through the principal thoroughfares was about twelve miles an hour. It was royal fun, and made
the right of way, but was risky business.

There is great excitability about a Russian. He loses his head
upon the slightest provocation. If you ask a drosky driver the second time how much his charges are he becomes excited and talks so
loud and fast that the people in the next block run to see who
is hurt.

I was driving one day down the principal street in St. Petersburg
with a member of the Privy Council. The carriage went at a rapid
pace. Directly we heard a great noise behind us. We looked, and
the people for two hundred yards in the street and on the sidewalks

in our rear were standing still and yelling at us. I asked my distinguished friend what the matter was. He replied that he did not know.

Our carriage rolled on at the same rapid pace. We didn't stop. Finally the confusion became so great that the people in front of us began to pause and gaze at us. The workmen who were putting down the Nicholson pavement on either hand stopped and yelled at us. Again I asked my friend what the trouble was, saying we were making a sensation. He looked around once more, and sure enough the whole great, broad street was full of people, directing their voices at our carriage. They pointed at us and made exclamations that even the native beside me could not interpret.

Five mounted policemen now turned into the street and began to ride us down. They cried, "*stoi!*" "*stoi!*" which means "stop."

Now my friend turned pale. He asked me if my passport had been returned to the hotel with the chief's signature—his leave for me to stay. I replied that it had been sent to the officer, but that as I had not received it I did not know if it was all right.

"I expect," said he, "that these officers are after you," and he called to the driver to *stoi*.

When the officers came alongside I unconsciously raised up, ready to be taken into custody, and looked to see which one had the handcuffs.

"See there!" exclaimed one of the mounted gendarmes.

My friend and I looked at the side of our horses, expecting to see signs of a crime, and saw a hold-back strap hanging loose! The driver got down and buckled the strap, the officers rode back; we drove on, and business in the Broadway of St. Petersburg was resumed.

It is no wonder that the poor, unschooled drosky drivers are unable to read their own language in print, as it is the most complex, complicated stuff ever concocted to worry a foreigner. In the first place, the alphabet has thirty-six letters, and nearly all the words are so long that the original design seems to have been to exhaust the alphabet as frequently as possible. In form the letters are akin to the Arabic, Greek, English and Turkish, while in sound they remind one of no other language. However, the Russians, considering their limited education, take an enviable rank in music and the arts generally. To the eye stupid, filthy, and slothful as a race, they have shown genius, neatness and energy in many individual cases.

No institution in the entire empire has suffered from the oppression of the despotism like the press. There are no real newspapers in Russia, on account of the illiteracy and the terrible censorship of the Tsar. In Moscow, with half a million of people, I doubt if there are 30,000 readers. When a newspaper publishes an article which reflects upon the crown or any official of the empire or member of the royal family, its publication is suppressed, its property confiscated, and its editor exiled. The effect is to caution writers and bring about security before an article is in type. So when anything is written for publication which the editor is not sure will pass the scrutiny of the censor, he first sends it to that official for examination. The censor is always busy, and ever deliberate. Sometimes he does not return a manuscript under a fortnight or three weeks, and seldom under a week. If it contains news, of course it is stale. But stale news is much preferable to the risks incident to unguarded publication. In Russia, as in all other countries, the best news relates to war, politics and government.

During my stay at St. Petersburg Katkoff, the world-famed editor of the Moscow *Gazette*, died. He was Tsar Alexander's counselor, and the English press commented upon his demise in an uncomplimentary manner. He was held responsible for much of the oppression, the absolutism.

All of these newspapers, when brought into the Russian postoffice, suffered at the hands of the censor. The offensive articles were obliterated. A printer's ink-roller was passed over the column, leaving it a dense black spot.

To get a cigar anywhere in Russia you must buy a whole box. It frequently happens, however, that the whole box contains but one cigar. Boxes are never broken, and the purchaser can make an examination of the weed only through the glass cover. You cannot tell till you buy and are permitted to break the seal just what the article is. Every box of cigars or cigarettes has a glass lid or cover, and you can see the article you purchase, but cannot feel or smell it.

Generally when you ask for a cigar a large box is handed to you. When you have selected the quality desired from a number of boxes laid out for inspection, you make known how many you desire and the dealer—the *tobac fabricker*—gives you a box containing the exact number. The boxes of one, two, three, five, six, etc., are made of every quality. Most of the cigars are very bad, the domestic manufacture generally intolerable, and the price is high.

This mode of guarding against evasions of the high taxes on cigars has been followed a long time. It grew out of the proposition laid down by Ivan the Terrible, Peter the Great and other Tsars, who held that all Russians were thieves and should be watched. I have heard a Russian proverb which declares that "our Saviour would rob also if His hands were not pierced." The guard kept over the sale of tobacco is extremely close. While nearly everybody smokes, very few chew, and chewing tobacco is rarely found on sale.

I have been in four or five of the largest banks in Russia, and many of the most extensive commercial and railroad houses, and nowhere have I seen figuring done by pen or pencil as it is done in America and England. The Chinese counting-machine, seen occasionally in the hands of John and Jap in the United States, is everywhere. If you buy a pair of socks for fifty copecks and a handkerchief for seventy-five copecks the shopkeeper, even the brightest, oldest and most experienced, has to go to his machine to learn the result—one rouble, twenty-five copecks. I venture that there are not a dozen bankers in Russia who would attempt to discount any draft, or issue a letter of credit, or change a ten-rouble note into copecks, without pushing back and forward for some time the strings of colored buttons in his machine, indicating numerals. But it is wonderful how adept some of them are in the use of the counting-machine. You may buy a bill of goods ever so large. The salesman keeps the machine beside him, pushing out the numerals as the purchases are made, and the instant you call for your bill he repeats the total. The Russians were taught most of their business knowledge by the Chinese and Turks, and these counting-machines are yet indispensable in all Oriental places of business.

In no civilized country on the face of the earth are more primitive implements in general use than in Russia. On one occasion I went around to a "machine shop." It was a place where all kinds of machinery are repaired and most of the domestic implements in common use are made. One of the principal pieces of machinery described and you comprehend the character of the establishment. An old-fashioned grindstone, four feet in diameter, was the "forger." While one man turned the crank which gave the stone revolutions, the other, seated above it, held on the implement in the course of repair or manufacture. In this manner axes, plowshares, scythe-blades, etc., were reduced and given shape and edge. The blast furnace was a simple pile of cinders, and the fire was kept aglow by hand-bellows operated by a small boy.

THE MACHINIST'S FORGE.

The same precautions against fire are taken in Moscow and St. Petersburg to-day that were in use a century ago. Scores of fire-towers are everywhere seen. They run up seventy-five to one hundred feet, are built like a light-house, with winding stairway, and have a platform all around at the top, where the watchman patrols, day and night. If a fire is discovered a signal is given and the fire department turns out. It was only recently that St. Petersburg, with hundreds of millions of Government property, secured a steam fire-engine. And this is a poor, old-fashioned affair. The hand-engine does service here yet, as in most other cities in the empire. When a fire breaks out the streets are cleared for such a department display as an American village would make ; people go wild, talk loud, get in the way, and when the fire burns out the fire department goes back to watch the towers for another signal.

The stranger wonders how, in St. Petersburg, for instance, the markets and shops are kept as clean as they are, when the water is so filthy. One can smell the water of the Neva, which furnishes the supply for drinking and household purposes, for a mile on an ordinary summer day. It discounts the water that used to get green in the Potomac flats at Washington. A native tells me the reason things are clean. Every day a health officer goes about inspecting the shops and houses. Gendarmes assist. If there is any stench or decay discernible, or any filth of any kind, the place is arbitrarily closed, and kept closed for weeks or months. There is no recourse, no help for it. Cleanliness in the commercial centers is an imperative necessity. Many people have been ruined in business by having their houses closed by the officers. They can never learn what is wanted. The reply is : "You must keep the premises clean." How clean is not explained.

Quite as suspicious means are employed in collecting the mails as in controlling the sale of cigars. A letter posted in a street-box is no more likely to come into the hands of the mail-carrier or collector than cigars are to pass through the hands of the vendor. The men who collect the mail have sacks of sheet-iron, which they first fasten under the street-box. Then they unlock the side of the box sufficiently to crowd in a small sheet-iron case. The latter pushes down and out the case containing the deposited mail, and it is locked. When the mail gets into the bag there are double locks and double security against theft by the collector.

The tax collector seems to be the only person the Tsar will in-trust with any of the many revenues of the crown. The mode of collecting and paying taxes in Russia and the basis upon which they are paid differ as far from those in the United States as can be im-agined.

Improvements are seldom made except by the noble families, who "stand in" with the crown and get exemptions. There is a revenue department, like the Treasury Department at Washington, and a retinue of collectors of internal, customs, and direct taxes. The people pay Government taxes direct, and a city tax also. The former is to the Government collector; the latter to those of the municipalities. The Governors of the cities—empire officers—disburse the municipal taxes as they wish, and being Government officers their funds are half interchangeable; that is to say, the funds of a city may be taken for the Government, but not *vice versa*. Thus, since the Tsar has no one to account to for disbursements, he may draw on the entire resources of his very great country when he wants funds for private or public purposes. There is no danger of being beaten at the polls for a second term or indicted for malfeasance in office, and it would be worth a life to hint at such a thing as dishonesty in Russian official circles.

Taxes are based upon the estimate of the collector as to what can be paid. There were appraisements of property, and there are appraisements yet. The lists of nobles, however, pay only enough to keep up the appearance of paying. The middle classes—those who have enough property in farms, etc., to make them a living when worked, and those who generally become Nihilists on account of the despotism—pay the burden.

The tax collector watches closely the property of these people, and if they reroof a house, paint, or build a new structure or a fence, a "reappraisement" is directly made, though the man may have just paid his taxes, and additional taxes are demanded. They must be paid instantly. The laws about confiscating property of persons who refuse to pay taxes are simply awful. If the property-owner makes any fuss about the matter he is classed as a conspirator, a conniver against the Government, and some fine day or night he is called upon by officers who look like innocent citizens. He leaves his family "to go to town," and next he is seen in the spirit land. He goes to the shooting-gallery or Siberia, where he is appointed to a position as marksman's target. He does not last long.

A Federal officer in the United States can trifle with the civil-service law with far greater safety than can a Russian speak of excessive taxes or delay when the amount is named.

Owing to this arbitrary and unjust system of taxation and discovery of improvements there is very little progress made. People never improve if they can help it. The principle upon which taxation and tax collection are based is suspicion. The Tsar believes his subjects are dishonest, and that they are ever trying to cover up their property. Under this system it is a wonder how shopkeeping and manufacturing are made to pay, and why Americans sometimes come to Russia to establish business. I so expressed myself to a cotton manufacturer, once a Bostonian, and he said :

"Americans and Englishmen engage in nothing in Russia unless there are enormous profits in it. The unprofitable business is left to natives, who do not understand our trade. I know a large manufacturer here who came from Massachusetts, whose works have been burned out almost annually, and who makes loads of money ; but the tax collectors don't know it, because they are ignorant of his affairs. They cannot comprehend a large business. You have no doubt discovered that all the shopkeepers have several prices for an article. It shows their desperation. They are driven to cheating and misrepresentation to come out even ; and the example is set by the highest power in the empire."

Since the determination of the Tsar to drive out all alien manufacturers it is not probable that the tax collector will long be in ignorance respecting the ways of the Yankee.

CHAPTER VIII.

HE Russians are proverbially fond of sports.

In some of the frigid regions they hunt the bear, wolf, elk, and many species of the smaller game, and gather in parties for the purpose, making their enjoyment a great social feature. The royalists, before so much feeling was engendered against the English, invited the subjects of the Queen to join them in their annual chase, and there were hunting parties of as extensive proportions as in other parts of the Continent.

There are armies of Siberian blood-hounds and the ordinary fox or wolf-hounds in every community. The peasants usually keep a pair of hounds for the purpose of driving off wolves, which are the bane of those who must cross the undeveloped country. Usually wolves appear in the greatest number in the improved country in the winter, and at times they gather in such large packs and become so fierce that great care must be exercised to keep them from devouring not only all of the live stock, but the people themselves.

Many times have thrilling stories been related to me of whole families being devoured by wolves, and even hunting parties becoming their prey. It is said that thirty or forty thousand people are killed every year in Russia by wolves; yet the Government takes no steps to exterminate them. In the region of Urkovsky wolves at times become so fierce that organizations of citizens turn out to slaughter them. Once there was a bounty of thirty copecks placed upon every wolf scalp taken in that district, and the stories which are told in St. Petersburg and Moscow of the slaughter that followed upon the proposition made by the Government are almost incredible.

Somewhere I have been told the story of a wolf-hunting expedition which is extremely thrilling, and which gives a pretty fair illustration of the average wolf-killing parties the Russians organize, with the assistance of visitors, almost every winter.

An American and an Englishman in one of the villages in the region of Urkovsky organized a wolf hunt, which in its results should go down to history, if the stories concerning it are true. The hunters had constructed a little house on runners. It was about the size of one of the photograph cars which are run through the United States on wheels and visit country places. In the structure were provided bunks, a stove, and other conveniences. Port-holes were on the sides and in the floor. The doors were made so as to slide. This structure was fitted up with fuel and provisions sufficient to last half a month.

Great curiosity and interest were shown by the natives of the village as the three men—the American and the Englishman taking with them a native—left the community and pulled their car into the very heart of the wolf country. They went right out on the plain ; were armed with shotguns and revolvers. It was in January, and the winter being severe the wolves were more numerous and voracious than ever before.

Raw meat was taken for bait, and a gallon of beef's blood was carried along. The latter, when the wolf region was reached, was scattered in the snow.

Finally the little car was stopped away out on the prairie, and two of the party went forth to sprinkle the blood on the snow and in trails, each one leading to the improvised fort. The details of this daring expedition are best told in the language of one of the men who participated in it.

"On our way back to the car," said he, "we left a bloody trail, and flung out a piece of meat at intervals. We had not yet reached the car when we heard the howl of a wolf, and in five minutes we could see a dozen of them scampering about. It was an hour, however, before one of them came within reach of our guns. Then the sun, which had been brightly shining all the forenoon, was hidden by clouds, and a snow squall came up to still further darken the heavens.

"The howling of wolves could now be heard in every direction, and pretty soon they followed the trail of blood in until we all got a shot, and each tumbled a wolf over. From the instant they fell to the time their bones were clean picked by their companions was not over forty seconds.

"It was something marvelous to watch the proceeding. The mouthful apiece whetted their appetites and stimulated their ferocity, and the whole pack made a rush at the car. The beasts no doubt took it for a travelers' sledge, and the attack was surprising in its fierceness. The number of wolves was not less than five hundred, and for the first five minutes we were seriously alarmed. They were over, under and around us, howling, barking, snarling, growling and fighting in a way to give us chills, and, had our car not been securely fastened to the broad, heavy runners, they would have upset it in their rushes. The exterior had been sheathed with sheet iron. We had objected to this expense, but had finally accepted the advice of one of the wolf hunters. We now realized the wisdom of this precaution. But for the sheathing the wolves would have eaten their way into the car in a dozen places.

"Such a fierce and unexpected attack rattled us for a few minutes; but after a bit we began firing buckshot into the pack as fast as we could load and pull trigger. Then it was pandemonium let loose. The howls, yells, yelps, growls and cries redoubled, because every victim of our guns was being devoured by his companions. We fired thirty-four charges of buckshot into the mass, killing at least double that number of wolves, and then the pack began to scatter, and ten minutes later not a living wolf was in sight. It was a horrible-looking scene around us. Every wolf but one had been devoured. Tufts of fur and bloody bones were scattered over the snow for a hundred feet in every direction, and there was not a foot of snow without its blood stain. There was a wounded wolf who had escaped the fangs of the pack, probably because their appetites were satisfied for the time being. He had been shot through the hips, and could no longer use his hind legs. He was a very lame fellow, and we soon had reason to believe that he was still dangerous. The beast was about fifty steps away when we descended from the car, and the minute he caught sight of us a great transformation took place. All the fur along his spine stood up, his eyes blazed like fire, and he uttered such fierce growls that the three of us raised our guns. The brute could drag himself over the snow crust with his forelegs, and as we stood looking at him he began hitching himself forward to attack us. We let him come within five or six feet of us before knocking him over. From his actions there is no doubt he would have boldly attacked the three of us had he been less desperately wounded. His scalp was the only one we saved out of the sixty or seventy shots. Not another wolf was seen until night came down. Then they gathered around us seemingly by the thousands. Looking out from one of the small sliding doors, we were reminded of a great drove of sheep cantering over rough ground. Not one of them was still for a minute, and a free fight was always in order.

"Our house stood six or seven feet high, and they leaped over it back and forth as easily as they could have cleared a log. At one time several of them engaged in a fight over our heads, and we had serious fears of the roof breaking under their weight. When we finally opened fire I honestly believe there were two thousand wolves within pistol shot. Our house was the center of a circle of leaping, howling, fighting, growling and yelping beasts, each one of which seemed bent on getting nearer. It was a bright moonlight night, and we did not waste a shot. One could have shut his eyes and been sure of killing or wounding at every discharge. We limited our shots to twenty-five each, and fired slowly so as not to heat our guns. I believe we killed a hundred wolves with the seventy-five shots. If one

was wounded enough to cause a flow of blood, the unwounded would
tear him to pieces with even more ferocity than they displayed toward
the dead. Soon after we had ceased firing the great bulk of the
wolves retired, to be seen or heard of no more during the night. A
few who had probably failed to secure a part of the horrible feast
remained in the vicinity to growl over the bloody bones and utter an
occasional howl, and after midnight we slept soundly.

"We were afterward told by peasants living eight or ten miles
away that packs of wolves passed their farms at dusk on the way to
the general rendezvous. Some of those surrounding our house probably came twelve or fifteen miles. The keeper of the hotel saw fifty
or more go by his place, and they were in such a hurry and so occupied
with the project on foot that they passed within twenty feet of a stray
colt without halting to attack it.

"On the second day of our stay we were witnesses of a dreadful
tragedy. It was a cloudy day, with occasional snow squalls, but no
wolves came near us. At about two o'clock, while my companions
were lying down, I opened the slide to take a look over the highway
toward Toblosky. For four miles the highway was over a plain, and
one could see every moving object. Then the road was lost in a pine
forest, which stretched along for a couple of miles. I had scarcely
pulled back the slide when an object came in view on the road at the
edge of the forest, and in half a minute I had made out horses. A
sledge was coming our way, the first which had passed since we took
up our station. We had a pair of field-glasses in the car, and I had
no sooner adjusted the focus than I uttered a shout which brought my
companions to their feet. There were three horses abreast, and they
were coming at a dead run, while on both sides of the sledge I could
make out fierce wolves jumping up. The team was a powerful one,
and coming very fast, and in a minute more I made out that the
sledge was surrounded by a great pack of wolves. The driver was
lashing the horses in a frenzied way, while the smoke and flame and
faint reports proved that the occupants of the sledge were using firearms to defend themselves. We had two or three minutes in which
to act. Each of us had the idea that the sledge would halt at our
car for protection, or that the people in it would certainly leap out at
that point. We opened one of the doors, got down our guns and all
were ready to leap out when a dreadful sound reached our ears. It
was the shriek of a horse. I say shriek, for it was nothing more nor
less—a shriek of terror and despair. The cause was plain when we

looked out. One of the horses had fallen when the sledge was hardly twenty rods away, and the other two had been dragged down with him. We could not see them, however, for the wolves. We just caught sight of two or three human figures in furs, heard the reports of pistols and shouts of human voices, and then the terrible din made by the wolves drowned all other sounds.

"We should have sprung out and gone to the assistance of the beset travelers, but before we could move foot our car was surrounded by wolves, and a monster got his head and shoulders into the doorway and hung there for a few seconds despite the kicks from our heavy boots. We opened the slides and looked out, but all was over then. The carcasses of the horses had been picked to the bone, the harnesses eaten, and the robes from the sledge were being torn apart as the wolves raced around. We saw pieces of bloody clothing scattered about, and we knew that the travelers had met a horrible fate.

"Afterward we learned that there were four men in the sledge. The pack of wolves, which seemed to be larger than any which had yet gathered, hung about until we knocked over at least fifty of them, and then drew off to return at midnight. We kept our position for nine days before the men would come with the horses, and, although we preserved the scalps of only three wolves, we estimated the number of killed at over eight hundred."

Besides the wolf chase there are gunning sports. Great parties of Russians frequently form colonies, and usually reside in portions of the country and engage in reindeer hunting. The encounters between the hunters and old stags and the battles with the grizzly afford an amusement the hearty natives greatly enjoy. The Russian knows no physical fear.

The markets are well filled during the summer and autumn with birds bagged by sportsmen in the vicinity of St. Petersburg. They have what corresponds with the American plover, partridge, prairie chicken and geese. There is a large following after the sports of Nimrod. With the exception of some scenes along the Seine, near Paris, I have seen more women and children fishing in the Neva than any other part of the world.

URING more than seven months in every year the entire face of the earth in Russia is covered with snow. The buildings are also covered with it, and the trees look like great stacks of snow. Were the trees of the heavy, broad-topped kind seen in America, they would all be broken down; but they are here very slender and afford little room for excessive weight.

Snow begins to fall around St. Petersburg early in September. Then the ground and water courses freeze, and do not thaw till May. Sometimes the snow covers everything for eight full months. The cold is terrible. The average temperature is what the Russians call "thirty degrees of cold," which means 30° below zero. Not infrequently it goes down to 50° and 55°, and I am told that every two or three years there is a cold snap, lasting from three to six days, when the spirit in the thermometer freezes. As this never happens until the temperature falls to 70° or 75° below zero, no one can tell exactly how cold it does get. It is then so cold you can see a glass of water when thrown out into the air freeze into ice before it strikes the ground.

An American going about the streets of St. Petersburg or Moscow during the frigid months is likely to have his nose or ears frozen. As these get dangerously cold they turn white, and the natives observing them will run up to you on the streets, slap your nose or ears, and tell you to go indoors. People dress in furs from head to foot. Great headdresses of furs, with long capes covering the face and shoulders, are generally worn. Holes are left for the eyes and mouth, and around the latter great cakes of ice form.

The first fall of snow is generally accompanied by winds which pierce one to the marrow. It makes a scene of desolation, leaving the tops of the little trees about the city uncovered, but carpeting the ground and buildings.

It is now that the preparations are made for procuring the supply of water from the Neva, as the river is frozen over and the water-works are closed. Those who carry their own water go to the river and cut and mark their holes in the ice. Water is carried in pails of Russia iron, the bale of which is caught in a notch of a long, swinging pole, and this rests across the shoulder, so that one person may carry two buckets. The water in the ice-hole instantly freezes when it is left undisturbed ; but sometimes a whole community uses one place, and, as it is kept in a turmoil during the day, freezes but little till night. A water-hole in the ice may get ten or fifteen feet deep before spring. The object in early cutting the ice for water is two-fold : the way to it is kept clear and the ice is not permitted to freeze so thick as it otherwise would. In many places in Russia the ice is ten feet thick.

Often people carry water for miles when the mercury is down to 30° below zero, and the contents of the buckets are solid masses when they reach their destination. But this may be a blessing in disguise. The Neva is a filthy river. The water is almost as dirty and smells much worse than that in the Chicago river in the metropolis of Illinois. The freezing and thawing processes have the effect of purifying and killing the animal life in it. A large proportion of the inhabitants of the principal cities are supplied with water by men who run water-carts. These consist of rough old vehicles with large barrels on them.

By the early part of October snow is so deep that farewell is bidden to all external views. People put on their snow-glasses to save their eyes, don the heaviest wearing apparel, and go about unbroken parts of the cities or country on snowshoes. If there have been heavy rains during the fall the ice crop may be gathered from the lowlands and streets on the level of the river—all is a glare of ice. If there were long and heated summers in Russia the ice crop would be an important one ; but as ice is only needed during three or four months in the year, not very much importance is attached to it. The ice harvest, however, takes place in the very heart of the cities, it being found in abundance everywhere. It is hauled to the houses, where it is stored, on sleds.

Winter is the gay season in St. Petersburg, and there is little doing in society till then.   The streets are kept as smooth as a floor by
immense bodies of laborers, who work day and night.   When a fresh
snow falls they roll it smoothly and compactly down on the principal
streets, so that early in the
morning, if the snow has
fallen at night, you can go
about with polished boots
and not get them soiled.
The rough edges and knobs
are cut down as carefully
as though the streets were
of everlasting stone, and
the shavings and pieces

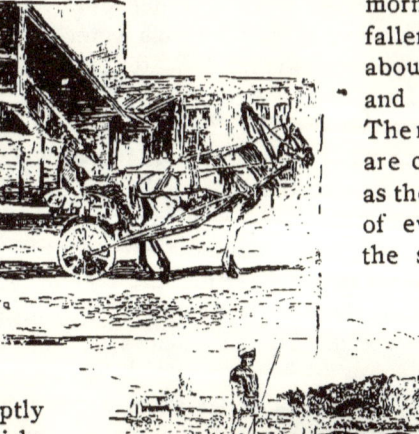

a r e   promptly
carted outs i d e
the city, l i k e
noxious garbage
in summer-time.
E v e r y b o d y
owns one, two
or three f i n e
horses, and
magnificent sleighs are as common as cutters in America.

It is in the winter that all the horse-racing takes place in Russia.
The rivers about the cities are the scene.   Many of the bridges are
pontoons and are taken down and put away as soon as the rivers
freeze, so that sleighs and sledges pass over on the ice without hin-
drance.   The ice is kept scrupulously clean, is smooth and level, and
horses trot down in the thirties and run in two minutes or less.   What
they could do on an ordinary race-track their owners do not know.
There is no racing in summer-time.

The popular amusement is sleighing.   It outranks all else.
There is no such thing as baseball here.   Occasionally there is a
game of cricket, and a few practice archery; but everybody goes
sleighing daily in the winter, and all who can afford it have horses for

racing. The turnouts in the summer on the boulevards at Chicago, in Central Park, New York, the parks in London and in the Bois de Boulogne or the Champs Elysees at Paris, are not to be compared to those seen in the streets of St. Petersburg or on the Neva in the winter. The horses here are the handsomest in the world—long, graceful blacks, with immense manes and flowing tails which sweep the ground, all perfectly clean and glossy. The sleighs are very beautiful, and are drawn sometimes by five horses abreast. Four horses to a sleigh are common.

When the snow disappears in the spring the streets present a horrid sight. The accumulations of seven or eight months are seen, and weeks of the hardest labor are required to remove them. It is then that the lazy, filthy Caucasian, perhaps from miles distant, comes in with his wagon and long-haired cows or steers to haul the garbage away. He puts up side-boards and takes an immense load of filth. He is paid two roubles a day for the work of himself and yoke of steers or cows ; but he gets the garbage for his master's land.

The streets are covered with boulders the size of a man's fist. The rock is laid down in the black mud, which works through ; and as the frost comes from the ground a terrible mess is the result.

The people in the country do not fare so well as those in the city during the winter. They have stock to feed and fires to provide. The sheds for the cattle are made of straw and poles, are low on the ground and generally comfortable. But a serious difficulty is encountered in securing water for the stock. Sometimes the wells and streams for miles are frozen to the bottom. In such cases the snow is melted, and the peasants drink this and eat dried fish and meats till whole families perish from scurvy.

Travel in the country during the winter months is almost wholly by means of snowshoes. The snow is so deep and the travel so infrequent that horses are not available. Reindeer and dogs are used when the snow gets a crust strong enough to bear their weight. Sometimes a sledge drawn by reindeer or dogs breaks through the snow and the party is not seen till spring, and then in a decomposed condition.

A more desolate scene cannot be imagined than a Russian village in January. The little straw-covered huts belch forth strands of smoke, and the tops can just be seen above the snow—or rather not the tops, but curvatures representing them. The horses, cows, sheep and family sometimes live under the same roof—no floor but the ground ; a poor, smoking, cold fire in the center of the hut, and men, women, children, dogs and all the farm animals huddling and shivering around to keep life and body together.

There is not a very pleasant atmosphere in the houses during winter time. The extreme cold requires the rooms to be almost hermetically sealed.

Nowhere are the windows in the houses made with a view to the American plan of ventilation. Instead of the sash sliding up and down it is stationary. They have in the right-hand upper corner of the lower sash one pane that opens out or in, and this furnishes ventilation. The sash, which is double and three or four inches apart is padded so it could not be opened if desired. The atmosphere gets so thick at times it can be seen.

All bedrooms are provided with two beds if two persons occupy them. Husband and wife even are separated. I presume this is because the foul atmosphere makes much restlessness. I know it was true with myself.

CHAPTER X.

OWEVER interesting the strange scenes in the streets of the cities may appear to an American's eyes, the sensation seems to increase when he emerges from the city and goes into the country to study rural life. Here are found more than three-fourths of the entire population. Only about two per cent. of the peasants can read and write, and few have the ordinary instincts of man or woman. They are superstitious, ignorant and stupid. But this is not to be wondered at. They have been a free people scarcely longer than the blacks of America, it being during the troublous slavery times in the United States that Alexander II. issued a ukase giving the white slaves of Russia freedom. They were not slaves in the sense of being owned, body and soul, by their landlords. The land which they occupied was the property of the nobility, and none were permitted, when once located on a farm, to leave it permanently or to go beyond a certain distance, even temporarily.

No schools were provided for the peasants during the time of slavery ; none are provided now, and then, as at the present time, the design of the Tsar, influenced by the nobles, was to keep them in the most dense condition of servitude and ignorance. Their earnings on the farms are gauged by the landlords, so they have just enough on which to live. As no means were provided for the elevation of the slaves when they became free, they have remained exactly where they were found, and for all practical purposes they might just as

well have remained slaves. It is generally believed that the Tsar's
act in emancipating them was to gain diplomatic favor abroad.

A peasant's house is a very rude structure and contains none of
the elements of comfort, healthfulness or cleanliness. His allowance
of furniture, food and clothing being fixed by the landlord, he lives
scantily. The building is usually of pine or cedar logs about ten
inches in diameter, barked and set neatly together. It is one story
in height, with one room, generally has three or four windows, with
one sash in each, and they are protected from the outside by rude
board shutters, which, when closed at night, make complete darkness within and ventilation miserable. The floors are of logs or
earth, and the beds are on the floor.

There are no stoves in a peasant's house. A stick-and-clay chim-
ney fireplace suffices. Here warmth is secured, and the food is
cooked in kettles. The family meal is spread on the floor and the re-
past eaten while sitting on folded legs, tailor style. In front of many
of these houses, which are covered with hay and poles—a rough sort
of thatch—the traveler frequently sees a drosky from the city, the vehicle of the landlord, who pays daily visits. The peasant has very
crude agricultural implements. He generally makes them at his own
furnace and gives them finish and polish on his own grindstone.
Axes, plowshares, wagon-tires, portions of harness, horseshoes, and
everything used about a farm or stable, are finished on the grindstone.

A crude little furnace heated with peat or pine chips and the
grindstone comprise the manufacturing appliances of the peasant.
His plow is a simple pole with handles on a dead level with the
tongue, which has an offshoot downward, on which the share is nailed
or tied.

A plowing scene in Russia, with the rough, old frame, the crude,
triangular or diamond-shaped share, and the tiny little furrow made,
would be disgusting as well as pitiable to the American farmer's eyes.
The draft or weight of the plow comes directly from the high-bowed
hames, which extend two feet above the horse's neck and are fastened
to the collar. Instead of traces, the tongue or shafts do the pulling.
The Russian in no walk of life has yet learned the philosophy of direct draft from the collar of the horse. All vehicles are drawn by the
shafts or tongues, and these are fastened to the high hames or bow,
which in turn are fastened to the collar. There are no such things as
trace-straps or chains. Even carriages are drawn without them.

The women in Russia do two-thirds of the work in the country.
There are immense wheat, oat and hayfields everywhere, and in Au-

gust there is great activity in the country. The large majority of persons at work are women. They wear short dresses, plain and straight, and a long piece of cloth over their heads, like Arabs. The wheat is sown broadcast, and if not cut by the women with sickles, is harvested with the old-fashioned scythe, which has a ten-pound snead and a broad, short blade. From the snead up to the handle there is a wooden bow, in appearance resembling half of a heavy barrel hoop. This bow keeps the wheat from falling back over the scythe-handle and scattering.

I have never yet seen a man who would deign to gather up, bind and stack the wheat or oats when once it was felled. The women must do this while the men do the easier work, although I have seen many women cutting grain with the scythe. The neighbors club together in harvest and help one another.

A Russian harvesting rendezvous is quite lively, and is the scene of a motley crowd. The old men and young boys and girls, with their mothers, grandmothers and other aged women, assemble at daybreak—about two o'clock. There are a number of horses, on which are carried water, food and extra implements. The horses the boys and men ride, while the old women walk. They always carry the scythes, forks and rakes back and forth every day, and work as long as there is daylight; and since it is daybreak at between two and three in the morning and not dark till ten o'clock at night, the hours of labor are long.

The forks used in the fields are made of the prongs of trees. A limb is selected which has at least three offshoots, and from this a hay or wheat fork is made. The wheat is stacked at first very like in America, except in the matter of cap-sheaves. Instead of three or four top-sheaves, just one is placed. It is turned heads down and spread so as to cover the entire stack. The heads of Russian wheat are long and slender and the grain small and red. It would be graded at Duluth or Chicago as No. 2. The straw is rank and slender, and the yield a little more prolific than in America. It is harvested and sown in the same month—August. When the wheat is sufficiently matured it is hauled on long, slender, one-horse wagons to the windmill on the farm and threshed.

The windmill which furnishes the flail-power for the threshing is of the same design as those found throughout Holland and Germany. It is double-armed—the same as the one Don Quixote set out to conquer. These mills are very common around Warsaw, and are used for every conceivable work, the women even grinding their coffee, churning and washing with them. The slightest breeze sets them going, as their faces are turned against the wind so as to catch its full force. This appears to be the only labor-saving institution found in Russia.

I asked a landlord why he did not introduce modern implements on his farms, and was informed that labor was too cheap; besides, it was found advantageous to give as many people work in the country as possible, because if they go to the towns or cities they become troublesome. It will not be till the serfs leave the farms that Russia will have modern improvements; and not till then will she compete to any great extent with the United States in supplying the wheat markets of Europe.

Although ignorant and kept away from general communication, the peasants in Russia are becoming greatly dissatisfied with the way they are treated by the Government and the landowners. They look upon the edict issued in August, 1887, upon the subject of education, as aimed at them more especially than at any other class. The Minister of Public Education declared that he would stop the last avenue possible to the education of the poor classes. His proclamation will not permit them to enter even the private universities, and closed the door of the public ones by a circular to the curators of the scholastic circuits, announcing that " the gymnasia and progymnasia will henceforth refuse to receive as pupils the children of domestic servants, cooks, washerwomen, small shopkeepers and others of like condition, whose children, with the exception perhaps of those gifted with extraordinary capacities, should not be raised from the circle in which they belong and thereby led, as long experience has shown, to despise their parents, to become discontented with their lot and irritated against the inevitable inequalities of existing social positions."

The real reason why this extraordinary proclamation was issued was the growth of Nihilism. This the officials freely and frankly admit. They say that as soon as the child of a peasant gets into school and begins to read and think he or she becomes a Nihilist and goes into the community whence the pupil came and spreads the infection. So the last channel to intelligence was thus closed. The edict was issued at the instance of the nobility and was intended to check the emigration from farms to the cities.

CHAPTER XI.

Village or commune life is also an interesting study in connection with the peasantry. Cities in the empire, as well as the country organizations, are ruled with an iron hand by the Tsar; yet those who chance to live in what are classed as villages have almost absolute local control.

Away back in the feudal ages, when the Tsar trembled for his power, there was established what is known as the law governing communities. A commune or community in Russia means a village corporation. The organization of a village for local self-government is as simple as its power when in operation is supreme.

GOING TO THE PEOPLE'S MARKET.

When a community concludes to organize a village for self-government a public meeting is called. An elder presides and states the object of the gathering. It is to elect a mir. A mir is a council or popular assembly of ten men. These are chosen from the body, like a committee on resolutions, and constitute a permanent court or tribunal for the trial of common causes embracing all penal offenses. Of course offenses against the Government or the crown do not come within even the preliminary jurisdiction of such legal bodies as these, for there is trial of such causes only by court-martial, which has no preliminary and no appeal.

The mir, or the village, at its meeting then selects a mayor, known as the starosta. This officer generally serves for the good of the community, without salary, for there is no tax or fund from which to pay him; and as no official return to the crown is made of these meetings and elections, there is no procedure for the collection by law of any debt on account of official services. The privilege of this form of self-government is simply vested in villages, and they may avail themselves of it, and once they do so they must settle questions pertaining to their organization themselves. There is no higher court to go to. Like the organization of Legislatures in the United States, the power of the body organization rests within the body itself.

There is a superstition that the power of the mir and the starosta is as divine as it is supreme. It is believed that these offices came down from God, as they afford the only channel for popular voice. When a village grows to sufficient importance to become, in the eyes of the Tsar, a city, a Governor is appointed. Then the Government, instead of the people, rules. The Governor of a city in Russia is closest to the crown, except members of the Cabinet; and he is always selected with reference to his loyalty to the Tsar. It is, for instance, a much greater thing to be the Governor of St. Petersburg, Moscow or Odessa than to be a member of an American President's Cabinet. The power is here supreme—never an appeal—the salary large, the honor to the limit, and the position for life.

Whatever the mir decides is settled. · The mir always concurs, too, in the decision of the starosta. If a popular question comes before the community, like that of some general improvement or the suppression of a local wrong, a public meeting is called and the starosta presides, while the mir sits in judgment like a jury. The verdict determines and there is no complaint at it.

To grumble at or question the verdict is to rail at the infallibility of the crown, which puts the dissatisfied in the light of an opponent to the Tsar, and he is at once detected, brought to St. Petersburg, and finally exiled to Siberia or shot at the Fortress, according to the gravity of his complaint. There is no mincing. Thus it is that the mir is not and yet is connected with the general Government of the empire. It is a purely local government, with the sanction and protection of the general Government.

Although the mir has power to do a great many things for the
good of the community, it cannot establish schools or churches, even
with its own money. The education and religion of the people are
the primary cares of the general Government. Churches are built,
supported and administered by the crown through a special tax which
all must meet.

Detectives and soldiers keep out contention and discontent, and
coerce the people into worship of a despotic general Government,
while the mir doles out justice locally. The inhabitants tremble
when they speak the name of the Tsar, and possess a holy fear of
and respect for him. Few travel beyond the confines of the commune, as all must have a new passport during January of every year.
This costs ten roubles, which is a heavy tax for the poor man with a
large family, every member of which must pay the tribute. Besides,
each passport must be *vised* by the local officer whenever the holder
desires to go outside the community. To this officer also must be
shown the object in making the journey. If it is ascertained that the
person who desires to go away is a malcontent or is suspected of conspiracy, he or she is detained. There are, therefore, no spreaders of
sedition roaming outside or inside the country.

Russian families are generally large. The children soon mature and are early earning their own livelihood. Many families consist of fifteen children. The infants are bandaged closely, like those of the Swiss, so as to prevent bow-legs ; and when they grow up for ten or twelve years are straight, well-developed, and are ready for the battle of life.

Some of the villages are peopled by gardeners and manufacturers, who supply the markets of the cities. There are markets here and at Moscow which are run almost solely by the villagers. The People's Markets generally mean markets by the producers, and are managed by those who live in the villages 'roundabout.

It is nothing for a villager to travel all night to market five roubles' worth of garden truck.

The transportation by the village marketman is through the medium of ox-carts. There is usually an open field hard by a city or a market where the peasant's oxen and cart stand during market hours. Sometimes one ox is hitched and the other loose, or one rests while the other munches grass. The cattle are generally poor in blood and flesh. Since the farmers of Russia are nearly all tenants, and the merchantmen who are not capitalists are serfs, the life of the villager appears to be the most contented and happy of all. He makes his own bed and he occupies it.

CHAPTER XII.

There is so much thievery in Russia that all the principal cities have what are known as Thieves' Markets. They are conducted openly, and little if any effort is made to trace an article which goes in that direction.

Travelers in their exasperation often declare that the authorities, the thieves, and the vendors of stolen articles, are banded together, and that the profits are divided on a fixed scale. Be that as it may, there is more stealing in this than any other country, unless probably Egypt is excepted.

In St. Petersburg the Thieves' Market is two blocks deep, four long, and gives commercial employment to thousands of persons. The goods are carried in by the pillagers, burglars and footpads, sold to the shopkeepers openly, and no secret is made of the fact that they were stolen. The buildings are mostly of brick, located in a quarter remote from the most respectable portion of the city ; and the shopkeepers live in the second stories. The rooms are all filthy, covered with vermin, filled with nauseous odors, and the goods are dusty.

Lazy men and women sit in front of the entrances to the shops in the narrow streets, play chess or cards, smoke, drink tea, and show a shocking degree of depravity. They are mostly Greeks, although many are Tartars, Jews and Egyptians. The Jews are said to be the most cleanly, honorable and intelligent.

The Thieves' Market flourishes most on a Sunday morning, although Sunday is not generally observed here, and street improvements, building of every character and trade go forward. But many people take a holiday on Sunday and spend it here. To this point I wended my way one Sunday morning, and saw a throng such as Five Points, New York, would have been shocked at in its palmiest days. In a window was some fine old chinaware, bearing the private mark of Alexander I., the crown and seal of the empire. Immediately the shopkeeper, a woman, informed me that the goods were stolen from the Winter Palace ; she knew it, because she got them directly from the thief, and she had handled his plunder before.

In the center of each block is a hollow square, about 150 feet in diameter. These were filled with men, women and children, behind improvised counters, selling or making almost everything. Second-hand boots are the most popular goods, and scores of men and boys can be seen repairing them in the open air, while others go about selling them.

HONEST MEN AND THIEVES.

The ground is bouldered and covered with sand and fleas. Pigeons and crows, both sacredly protected, hop about everywhere. The crows are dark gray, with little black coats. Great big Siberian hounds, muzzled, stalk about with the multitude and give zest to the scene.

Here are train-loads of old iron, copper and leather; hoops, cast-off and new clothing; jewelry, watches, clocks and silverware; furs, everything that furnishes houses, man, woman, child and beast, in confusion and profusion, just like a heap of stuff a gang of burglars might drop when hotly pursued.

It is said the thieves linger here after disposing of their plunder, often succeeding in regaining the property when it is purchased, and that goods are stolen and re-stolen a number of times in a single day or night. The scenes about the Thieves' Market in St. Petersburg are duplicated in four or five places in the empire. They are as old as the cities, having become fixed institutions, and no attempt is made to break them up.

It is related that Peter the Great, once remarking to a guest upon the propensity of his subjects to steal, observed that in the midst of prayer at church a Russian would not hesitate to rob his neighbor.

The inclination to steal varies in the classes only according to opportunity. Officials who pilfer do it in a more civilized and respectable way than the common herd.

I have heard a story about Russian thieves which illustrates their dexterity as robbers. A French noble who had suffered much from thieves at St. Petersburg made a wager with a member of the royal family that he could produce Russian thieves who would rob a man at the dinner-table, and he might use every precaution to prevent it. To the dinner a number of guests sat down. The royal Russian naturally supposed that one of those who sat about the board was the expert thief, and to them he directed his attention.

From the prison one of the most hardened rascals was taken and told that if he would rob the Grand Duke he should have his liberty. The thief was dressed as and acted the part of lackey and waiter. The liveried servant moved about with all the grace and pomp of a lord. Indeed, he so little resembled the adroit rogue he was that his employer began to fear as the dinner progressed he had made an unwise selection.

It was arranged between the master and the thief that when the latter had accomplished his difficult mission he was to indicate it to the former by a sly wink.

The wine flowed, the soup, fish, meat, game, the various entrees and relishes appeared and disappeared ; and still no signal of success.

Finally the cigars were passed, and as they were being lighted the thief gave the signal. The master asked his guest the time of night. The guest, with pleasing confidence, drew his guard, and found at the end of it, instead of his watch, a slice of turnip.

Then the host asked his guest for some snuff. The box was gone. Inquiry was made for a beautiful ring which the guest had worn. That, too, was absent. His purse had likewise disappeared.

But the most astonishing part of the performance was discovered in the fact that not only had the guest of the evening been robbed, but the host likewise.

So helpless are the honest natives when robbed that they often seek witches to trace the direction of the stolen property. The witch proceeds by peculiar means. She summons all the neighbors whom she suspects, gets a pail of water, makes a little roll of dough to represent each one present, and begins in the presence of the party to drop the balls into the water, the theory being that when she names the thief the ball will sink.

Nine times out of ten the witch forces a confession. It is a waste of time to appeal to the authorities. The superstitions of the people are thus turned to advantage. They believe it is far worse to be detected in crime than to make a free confession.

In nearly every bedroom I have occupied in the Russian hostelries I have found a tiny shrine. Some are over the doors, others high up in the corners next to the ceiling, while a few are stowed away on top of wardrobes. The presence of the shrine is not only a satisfaction and a solace to the occupant of the room, should he be a Russian, but a protection to the landlord, for it has not been frequent that thefts are perpetrated in the presence of shrines. The thieves fear shrines more than the law.

Laws may be enacted and punishment provided which will cure the Russians of their thievery, but only education and a change in the form of government can eradicate some other evils. The Russians are the most persistent drunkards I have ever seen. The ambition of the men of all classes seems to be to get money enough to supply them with vodka, a native corn brandy, which intoxicates as quickly as the worst kind of American whisky, and must leave a terrible effect. I am told that the peasants are becoming so debauched that they spend most of their church festival days in drunken ribaldry— and the Church of Russia makes about sixty holidays in the year. The church member must fast, must abstain from meat, but he may get as drunk as a lord and make the air resonant with his unmusical voice.

One of the most lamentable features in the multitude of sinful practices of the Russians is the moral support given to the bearing of illegitimate children. In the eyes of Russia and Russians it is neither disgraceful nor sinful, nor is it unlawful, for a girl to become a mother when unmarried. The Emperors of old set the example and fixed the standard within respectable limits. Catharine II., who rode horseback like a man and commanded or reviewed her own troops, and who likewise committed various indelicacies during her reign at Moscow, founded a magnificent hospital. She set up a code of rules for its government, which are in full force to-day, and which simply give a premium to illegitimate childbirth. And under the fast-and-loose regime of the country it is hardly necessary to observe that this institution is well patronized ; not only this one, but the various others which have been founded upon a like principle.

At the Moscow hospital alone between three and four thousand children find a home annually. It is a magnificent structure, with a dowry from the empire. No questions are asked when admission for a foundling is desired ; and further than this, means are provided for not only receiving the foundlings without disclosing the identity of the mothers, but provision is made for accouchements.

There is also a private entrance to this hospital, where, at any hour of the day or night, a child may be brought, deposited in a basket, and by an automatic process carried to the reception-room. The messenger may depart unseen and unknown. A ticket is placed in the basket, stating the date of birth and the name desired for the infant.

The little one is examined, weighed, registered, taken to the chapel, and immediately baptized and assigned to a nurse. It is given the best attention, and can be taken away after five years by any one who claims it, and besides receive a dowry till it becomes of age.

If the child is a female and is reared in the hospital till of age or grown, every effort is made to wed her to a creditable man. She is educated, shown about, dressed well, and receives a dowry at the marriage altar. She is of age when eighteen. The boys are liable to military duty, and are dismissed with thirty roubles and a suit of clothes when they become eighteen.

Some women who bear illegitimate children and do not want the fact known for some reason aside from the public notoriety, have an interesting way of rearing their offspring in a foundling hospital. They first mark the children by tattooing at a point where it will not be discovered upon a cursory examination. Then they deposit the children by the secret process at the hospital and engage as nurses. Once in the employ of the hospital, they not only manage to nurse their own offspring, but they receive better remuneration than were they employed as domestics in private families. This practice is so common that the authorities in charge of these hospitals prefer to employ women believed to have children in the institutions, through a sense of sympathy and because the mothers put more heart in the work.

Thievery, drunkenness and patronage of the foundling hospitals are not the only sins of the average Russian. The shopkeepers, as a class, need watching by the customer. When asked why there was so much cheating and misrepresentation among the higher class of Russian merchants, one of them whom I became well acquainted with said :

"There is so much oppression of the trade by the authorities—such high taxes, such stringent regulations—that every subterfuge is resorted to in endeavors to make a profit. You will find that it is not so much what is asked for a thing as it is what the shopkeeper thinks you will pay. Bid down every one, and keep a sharp lookout that you get what you buy."

So much roguery and oppression is everywhere found, and so many anticipate a climax to and an end of it all in revolution, that poverty is the rule. The lower and ignorant classes cannot be so much blamed for their reckless immorality when they have such glaring and bold examples from the nobility and the educated. For more than a thousand years the country has been ruled by persons who committed crime for amusement, and who believed that crime could only be atoned for or punished by crime. It has been a continuous page of blood, suffering and oppression, and the thing is a part of the bone, blood and flesh of this generation. So much for the bad people of Russia.

CHAPTER XIII

OVING bodies of troops in any section of the empire are invariably preceded by a strong skirmish-line of Cossacks. This branch of the soldiery is picturesque in the highest extreme and dashing to the limit of imagination.

During the palaver in the winter of 1887-8 between Germany and Austria on the one side and Russia on the other over the occupation of the throne of Bulgaria, the Russian frontier swarmed with mounted Cossacks. They dash over the country like a pestilence, and to the inhabitants are as cankers or parasites. There is nothing that will chill the blood quicker or more thoroughly than the thought of having located about a community an army of these men, who are without conscience or fear, who are licensed marauders, and whose reward is their pillage.

There is nothing found in any soldiery of the world that is akin to the characteristics of the Cossacks. The Cossacks are individually civilized, but collectively are as barbarous and ferocious as the Arab warriors in the Soudan. The presence of a body of Cossacks is always regarded as ominous. What with the students' outbreaks in St. Petersburg and Moscow, the menacing messages from the countries to the north, northwest, northeast and east, Russia for years has had much to agitate her; and the constant activity on her frontiers and in the War Office has been enough to unstring the nerves of most nations.

In the streets of St. Petersburg one usually sees but few soldiers, and most of them are the Cossacks, who are the Life Guards of the Tsar. Such universal prestige attaches to this soldier that many of the ordinary regulars attempt to imitate him. The genuine Cossack has no more appreciation of danger in battle or elsewhere than he has of his vodka, the terrible rum which he drinks like water, and which almost intoxicates at sight. The Cossack, besides being the original soldier of Russia, is the patron detective and the all-powerful police spirit. He assists in coercing the population into bearing the present iron rule and in making imperial institutions what they are.

The Russian army, according to the most accurate statistics obtainable, consists of 43,400 officers, 1,989,493 men in the rank and file, 318,852 horses and 3,794 guns. The reserves of the empire amount to over 3,000,000 in the rank and file, over a half-million horses, and about 4,000 guns. This makes a grand total of over 5,000,000. The cavalry figures do not show the effective strength of Russia in that branch of her army. Readily she may add half-a-million mounted effectives to the number given. Russia can mobilize forces within three months, at any time, aggregating 3,000,000, of whom one-third will be available as cavalrymen or infantrymen. The discipline and general worth of the Russian soldier are not excelled even by Germany, with her almost perfect army. The Russians boast that they can call into the field an army in less than a year of 8,000,000 soldiers; and I do not doubt this estimate, considering that she has 100,000,000 population, and allies with almost as many souls. The French are among the allies of Russia, and the Italians and Swiss are more than ordinarily friendly.

The navy is in proportion to her army. The empire has recently constructed some of the most formidable men-of-war to be found anywhere. The last warship built for Russia is said to be the largest and most nearly invulnerable of any in the world. It cost over four million roubles, and has secret designs which the architect refuses to disclose and the crown will not permit to be made known. I made strenuous efforts, with the use of letters from prominent American officials, to secure admission to this magnificent man-of-war at St. Petersburg, but was refused even a near approach.

The soldiers of Russia are largely garrisoned about the cities, and are frequently used for police duty in suppressing riots, patrolling places supposed to be in danger and preserving peace. The laws of the empire are applicable in the government of cities and villages, and the officers of the municipalities and the army are closely allied. There is not, however, the display of soldiery about the streets that one sees in some other countries on the Continent. For instance, one never encounters squads of troops moving in the streets as he may in Switzerland, Italy and Germany. They are kept in the barracks, and when permitted to go out they move about singly, and not collectively, and as warriors.

During my stay at St. Petersburg I visited one of the summer rendezvous of the army, about thirty miles to the east. There were sixty thousand soldiers in camp, and the occasion of my visit was to witness one of the memorable sham battles these soldiers frequently indulge in.

I saw a bombardment in which were engaged eight regiments. Six regiments of infantry attempted to take a breastwork occupied by two regiments of heavy artillery. The battle-ground was five miles in diameter. The breastwork was located at one side and against a wood. The skirmish and the repulse, the final charge and the capture, were pronounced by a veteran who accompanied me as lifelike as could be produced. There were clouds of smoke hovering over the field for hours after the engagement; and subsequently and in the midst of it was a terrific fight between the cavalry and the Cossacks. The latter held a small wood almost in the center of the field, and mounted cavalry and cavalry on foot attempted to dislodge them. There were fighting with sabers on horseback, hand-to-hand engagements on foot, and running firing from horseback and on foot alternately.

The style of warfare the Cossacks pursue is in many respects similar to that of the North American Indian. They are magnificent horsemen, are as tough as knots, and as bold as lions. The battles were reviewed by Tsar Alexander's brother, the Grand Duke, who is the General of the army. He is a splendid specimen of physical and mental manhood, thoroughly educated, and courteous to everyone. The soldiers love him dearly, and I do not wonder that they do, for he takes as good care of them as his resources will permit. As the long lines of troops hurried past the commanding officer every head was bared and in chorus the soldiers sang out their compliments, to which the Grand Duke replied most affectionately.

The manœuvres of the Russian soldiery are exceedingly attractive—made so by the great variety of uniforms in the ranks and the styles of arms and equipments worn. The artillery, infantry, cavalry and Cossacks are all uniformed and armed differently. One cannot imagine a more thrilling sight than five or six regiments of mounted Cossacks, with their breech-loading repeaters across their backs, immense revolvers in the pommels of their saddles, their long, steel-pointed spears, dashing across an open space and yelling like Comanches. It would seem that an ordinary stranger would be almost willing to give up his life without a struggle, if he were to meet one of these remarkable cavalcades of warriors.

FIRST OF THE PACK TRAIN.

Besides the license for crime issued to the Cossacks, by complete immunity from punishment for any misdemeanor committed, there is another great injustice done in relation to the army.

The commissions are given to the nobility. Spurs are never won by gallantry in the service. The noble families support the Tsar, and their sons take the honors in the military line. I remember to have seen a boy—surely not over eighteen—with a Colonel's epaulets and saber, reviewing the exercises, while many boys wore the stripes of

Captain and Major. To their commands grim veterans, who fought in the Crimea, responded with alacrity.

Despite the fact that the pay of the officers and privates is nominal, Russia's daily expenditure for her army is over two million roubles, while the cost of her navy more than exceeds half this amount.

There are enough horses and mules connected with the Russian army to fill the standing room of a section of land ; while hundreds of trains would be required to transport the arms of men used. Down on the Volga and in the country about Odessa camels are used in many instances as pack animals for the army.

The system of conscription during times of war or threatened war, or when the army has been reduced by desertions, is terrible. No man or boy who can bear arms escapes. During the last war of Russia there could scarcely be found an able-bodied man in all the country who was not doing service for the Tsar.

Necessarily this leads to many desertions. Added to the hated force which permits no man to escape military service, there is disagreeable monotony in army life. Even those who have families are never given leave to visit their homes, while the unmarried men are expected to serve the longest enlistments without seeing kith or kin. When the ranks are recruited by exercise of the conscript laws the scenes at the rendezvous where regiments are made up and hurried to the front beggar description—mothers, wives, sisters, soldiers, in tears at a parting which may be forever. It is far different from serving under the rules and regulations in the army of the United States, where there is such a thing as a furlough, sick leave and assignment in a public place, where the soldier is permitted to go and come at will among his family.

Prior to the Crimean war it was customary among the landowners to send worthless characters to the army, to get rid of them. When a slave was threatened with army service he was usually possessed of energy, better character, and any quantity of fear. If his master said, "I will make you a soldier," the fellow fell upon his knees and begged for dear life.

A deserter receives rough treatment when captured. I remember. to have been at the station one afternoon when the train arrived with a deserter aboard. As he emerged from the carriage there was heard a clanking of chains; and then appeared a poor fellow with hands tied behind him and feet hobbled. Four soldiers guarded him. One walked on either side, one in front, and the fourth in the rear. Each guard had his bayonet fixed, and it was pointed within close proximity to the deserter's person. Outside the station he was hustled into a drosky, was immediately surrounded by a whole company of soldiers, with bayonets fixed, and as the procession moved through the streets a scene was presented which, although it attracted no attention from the natives, suggested that a number of most dangerous criminals were in custody.

The conscriptions have had the effect of ridding the streets of loiterers and keeping the country free from mischief-makers; but they have surely not had the effect of elevating the character of the men in the ranks.

A Russian veteran tells me that the bivouac of an army corps in winter-time is the most distressing scene the eye can compass. The men often camp outdoors, when the mercury registers thirty degrees below zero. They are frequently seen stretched out on the ground before fires, fast asleep, during the day, and at night they walk in circles to keep from freezing. When morning comes the men fall into line at the tap of the drum or the bugle's blast, and singing the war-song of the Russian army appear the very essence of cheerfulness. They go into action believing that if it is willed that they shall fall they will fall, and that if they are to come out unharmed it will be so, and individual action has nothing to do with it. In short, they believe in foreordination.

Even a sketchy account of a trip through Russia would not be complete without reference to that page in the history of the empire upon which is written the record of the conflict known as the Crimean war.

This fact was brought more forcibly to my attention when I visited the War Department in Washington a few days ago and had pointed out to me one of the messengers of the Surgeon-General's office, Captain Thomas Morley. Morley is about fifty-six years of age and has the air of a veteran about him. The events in which he took a prominent part when the writer of this was still unborn have been chronicled by Tennyson in his celebrated poem, "The Charge of the Light Brigade."

Morley was but eighteen when he enlisted in the British army, was assigned to duty in the Seventeenth Lancers, and it is thirty-four years ago now that his troop, numbering one hundred and forty-five men, formed the last squad of the Earl of Cardigan's Light Brigade, which charged the Russian lines at Balaklava. Of the one hundred

and forty-five an even hundred were left on the field.   Morley himself was wounded twice, but not so severely as to incapacitate him
for further service after the end of that campaign.   At the close of
the Crimean war he returned to England and remained until hostilities
broke out in the United States, when, one day meeting Major-Gen-
eral Charles Havelock, who was coming to this country as inspector
of cavalry, he accepted an invitation to accompany him.   He was
commissioned as Second Lieutenant in a Pennsylvania regiment, and
rose to the rank of Captain.   He saw heavy service in the United
States, but nothing to compare with the charge of the Light Brigade.
He had two horses killed under him, was twice captured, and one
time confined for a year in Libby Prison.   He is a quiet, sedate man,
who has the respect of all his associates, and is often asked to give
some of the details of the famous charge in which he participated.

This has been graphically described by an English General who
witnessed the charge.   This officer thus states his recollection of that
thrilling event :

"On October 25, 1854, our eyes turned to the heights of Balaklava, on the possession of which depended the very existence of the
allied forces.   On that day the Russians made a desperate attack on
our lines, to be as desperately repulsed.   Word was sent to headquarters that the enemy, under cover of a heavy fire from the forts, had
left Sebastopol in force, and was massing himself so as to threaten
the safety of the heights.   I was at once sent with an order for the
cavalry and horse artillery to move, and be ready to assume the offensive.   They had not to wait long.   The Turkish lines were swept
as by a whirlwind, and with our Mohammedan allies the word was
sauve qui peut.   The heavy cavalry on the right and the Light Brigade on the left were advanced, with the artillery in the center playing a game at long bows.   Meanwhile a Russian battery was ostenta-
tiously moved forward, whose well-served guns promised to be em-
barrassing.

"Lord Raglan, who did not know the full strength of the foe,
saw that this obstacle must be removed ; but whether or not he also
foresaw the necessity of first looking before the leap was taken must
be forever a mystery.   The commanders of the cavalry brigades,
Lords Lucan and Cardigan, brothers-in-law, between whom no love
was lost, were waiting the word to engage, Lord Lucan being the se-
nior officer.   To them sped Captain Nolan, a dashing hussar.   Sa-
luting the General, he said he bore an order—unwritten—from Lord

Raglan that the battery must be silenced and the guns captured. Lord Lucan, a man so cautious as to have earned the nickname of 'Lord Look On,' fearing to expose his small force to any ambushed dangers, asked for more definite orders. With a slightly contemptuous turn of his handsome lip, the aide-de-camp pointed in the direction of the battery and said:

" 'You see your enemy, my lord.'

"Even the Earl of Cardigan, impetuous as he was, generally speaking, looked at his commander in doubt as to the words. But, owing to the unhappy enmity existing between them, neither would speak his thoughts, and once more Nolan, impatiently waving his sword, which he had fiercely drawn from its scabbard, and pointing it to the artillery, cried, 'Take the guns; these are your orders!'

"The crisis has arrived. No recourse is left but to do as he bids. A cold nod of assent from Lord Lucan. A profound bow follows from Lord Cardigan. 'Light division, forward, charge!' breaks from his lips. An echoing cheer is the reply from six hundred and seven throats, as with clang of scabbard and rattle of bridle and bit, and the braying of the trumpet, and the ringing cheer of the 'Heavies,' the Fourth and Thirteenth 'Lights,' the Eighth and Eleventh Hussars, the latter Lord Cardigan's own corps, conspicuous in their cherry-colored trousers, and the Seventeenth Lancers, with ranks closed up and squadrons dressed as evenly as if at a march past, trot forward down the slight declivity. At their head ride the gallant Nolan and the dauntless Cardigan, even in this supreme moment with a reckless laugh upon his face as he argues some point of war with his brother hussar.

"The unmasked batteries are already belching forth shot and shell. The trot breaks into a gallop—the gallop into a furious, headlong charge. Already Nolan has fallen, cut down by grapeshot, the secret of the fatal day dying with him. The serried ranks show frequent gaps, as saddle after saddle is emptied. 'Close up! Close up! Charge!' is the unceasing cry; and in a shorter time than it takes to tell the opening ranks of the foe disclosed to the doomed but indomitable few cannon to right of them, cannon to left of them, cannon in front of them—and now cannon behind them. On through the broken Russian line pressed the noble army of martyrs, their oriflamme, their brave leader's flashing saber, their support.

"With a wild cheer and a wilder leap, the cherry-clad heroes fly over the guns as lightly as they would over a five-barred gate on the hunting field, sabering the gunners as they leap. A beardless boy, not yet seventeen, holds fast to the colors he has sworn to carry to death or victory, and falls with the cry, 'My mother will hear of this!' on his dying lips, still grasping that banner in his hand.

"Far away, clear in front, with his aide-de-camp and a few choice spirits on his right hand and on his left, none ahead of him, raging like a lion, fights, as with a forlorn hope, the leader and commander of the Light Brigade. He bears a charmed life, and his brawny arm is endowed with a power of slaughter that grows mightier every moment from the meat it feeds on. Further and further he dashes on, cleaving his way with his blood-stained sword, till he reaches the last of the guns.

"Here, when he sees the end is not yet, but that rank upon rank of infantry and cavalry, with heavy artillery in the rear, stretches out back to the city's utmost bastion, he recognizes how useless it will be further to tempt the fates and fight one against a thousand. Coolly and calmly, as if in Hyde Park, he takes in the situation at a glance, and gives the word to the trumpeter to sound first the 'assembly,' then the 'retreat.' A bullet crashes through the boy's hand as he raises his trumpet to his mouth, but, stoic-like, he makes no sign. Clear rings out the summons. A dozen only answer the call. Not one, save Lord Cardigan, but is wounded more or less severely, and his clothing shows where lance or saber or ball had plowed its way over his unscathed flesh. Right about the little band turns, leaving the boy trumpeter dead on the ground behind them.

"The enemy, paralyzed by the shock of the charge, and fancying that the whole British army supports the handful of braves, pauses in his murderous work to cheer the one hundred and eight survivors who returned slowly and sadly to the place from which they came, having, from a military standpoint, achieved nothing, yet covered with a deathless, fadeless wreath of glory. 'It was magnificent,' said General Bosquet, 'but it was not war.'"

CHAPTER XIV

There is but one regular passenger train each day between St. Petersburg and Moscow. The distance is about the same as that between Washington and New York or New York and Boston, which is made in a little over five hours by the American railroad system. It takes fourteen hours in Russia to cover this distance.

Great is the circumlocution in securing a berth in the one *wagon lit* which runs between the two cities. It is an abbreviated pattern of the Mann boudoir car, and is quite as comfortable and sightly. The sleeping-car is a new thing here, and is only patronized by strangers and a very few of the most enterprising and wealthy natives.

The regular express leaves St. Petersburg at 8.30 at night and arrives at Moscow between ten and eleven o'clock the next forenoon. Two days before I departed from the Capital, with the courier I went to the station to procure a sleeping-car ticket and engage my berth. After unusual palaver the outer guard admitted us into several rooms and into the office of the agent.

At a desk I found an enormous Russian, apparently six and a half feet high and two and a half feet across the chest, with boots the tops of which came above his knees, and a beard as long and broad as the page of an ordinary newspaper. I had paid eighteen roubles for my railroad ticket to Moscow—about one-third more than the charge for the distance in the United States—and I was informed that a berth in the *wagon lit* would be an additional tax of ten roubles.

When the money was counted out to the agent he proceeded to open a blank book and fill out a page quite as large as a sheet of foolscap paper. This he handed to me, saying that it was a receipt for my money, and that it would guarantee a berth on the day after to-morrow. He added that when the train was ready to start he would give me a ticket for the receipt. Just why I could not get a ticket instead of the receipt, as in the United States and in the Continental countries, I could not understand and do not now know.

The evening arrived when I was to leave for the old Capital. The porters in the hotel visited my room early in the morning and expressed regret that they were to lose a guest. Their evident sorrow was soon palliated by a two-rouble note for each one, and they bade me good-bye with unmistakable evidences of happiness.

Here, as in many cities on the Continent, you settle your hotel bill every day, if you wish. Each morning a bill for your room and the etceteras is presented. This is charged up, but the landlord does not expect its liquidation on the day it is rendered. It is for the purpose of keeping you well informed of the aggregate of your expenses, so that corrections may be made if necessary while the items are fresh in your mind. Your carriage bills, expenses for couriers, etc., are charged with your room rent if you desire ; but your meals are paid for, usually, at the time they are taken.

After a great ado at the hotel in the settlement of every conceivable bill and satisfying the hints for tips from nearly everybody connected with the institution, I was off to the station.

About the door of the sleeping-car agent's office were congregated several travelers, all clamoring for berths. Great were my amazement and chagrin when I was told that I could not procure a ticket for the *wagon lit;* that the seats were all taken, and, in fact, several more were sold than were at the disposal of the agent. However, I produced my receipt, showing that I had paid my money two days since ; and after the courier threatened to call the gendarmes and arrest the agent, he was coerced into depriving somebody of his berth and giving me the ticket I was entitled to.

There is no drinking water to be procured on one of these trains, and the wise man takes with him a quantity of mineral water. In every other part of the country there are water vendors at almost all the stations ; but as this trip is made mostly at night these water men and women are not encountered.

One of the most striking features to an American in traveling through Russia is the utter lack of happiness found everywhere among the natives. There is never a merry laugh or a pleasant smile on the faces of the people who were reared here. Grim care and deep wrinkles occupy almost every countenance. The children appear as wretched as the parents, and are never seen rollicking about on the lawns or romping through the streets. They move around, as little pieces of machinery, in a mechanical sort of way. This is not owing to a lack of cultivation and improvement of the natural surroundings. There are around Moscow many pretty homes and beautiful lawns, which would bring pleasure to the children and real happiness to the parents in other climes.

The Russians are, in many respects, like the North American Indians. They are extremely stoical, fearless, superstitious and serious. They never see any fun in anything. Every effort made by my companions and myself to amuse the natives proved fruitless. A Russian does not enjoy a story, sees nothing humorous in pranks, and takes everything as a matter of course.

In skurrying through the country one travels over hundreds of versts sometimes before he finds an attractive place, such as are seen in the rural districts of the United States. There are no grand old plantation places—beautiful mansions surrounded by groves and attractive out-houses, walks and fountains. The landlords almost invariably live in the cities, and pay frequent visits to their estates. The homesteads of the aristocracy are found in the larger places, and not in the country. The provincial towns are quite as tiresome, when the novelty wears off, as the pine woods, marshes, and long stretches of barren country.

The traveler distinguishes a village from a city some time before he reaches it ; and he can never be mistaken if he once sees only the outskirts. The private houses in the cities have green roofs, and the churches and public buildings have gilded domes. These are never found in the small places.

When the train pushes into a post-station there is not the animation evinced in other countries. A crowd of natives move almost lifelessly about or stand still, gaping at the passengers or the train. The men have their hands rammed down into their breeches pockets, and are generally puffing strong clay pipes, and gazing intently, without evidence of spirit. The women, with 'kerchiefs tied over their heads and under their chins, give proof of quite as much interest in the proceedings, but usually are content with ogling and resting their hands on their broad hips. They have downcast looks, inexpressive faces and cowed manners, as though they were shrinking from an uplifted lash.

I have described the home of the peasant—its unattractiveness, unhealthfulness and filthiness. Mark the contrast in comparison with the mansion of the nobleman, who owns the land on which the peasant lives.

The mansion, to begin with, is larger, in most instances, than those found in America. There is a loftiness seen nowhere else ; and the furniture is selected with a special view to grand receptions and entertainments of every description. The floors are seldom covered with carpets. They are made parquet, or of inlaid oak. Not infrequently each room in a large mansion has a floor of a distinctive design. The doors are wide and are shaded by rich portieres to match the window curtains of the room. Magnificent chandeliers are suspended ; the ceilings are richly frescoed, and the gilt is used to splendid effect. Velvet or brocaded silk of the most delicate and fascinating colors covers the sofas, chairs and *tctc-a-tctcs*. Marble statues, exquisite vases, objects of *virtu*, and the oddest *bric-a-brac* to be found anywhere, are on every hand. The boudoir of the lady of the house is generally a perfect gem, with its furnishings profusely covered with delicate blue or rose-satin brocade. It may be that the floor is partly covered with a genuine Persian carpet. On the table is solid silverware, with the Russian enamel, which is the most perfect I have ever seen. Paintings decorate the walls, and there is an *abandon* in the artistic effect of the whole arrangement of the mansion that must be admired by every one.

The wives and daughters of the Russian nobles wear the most valuable and often the most gaudy jewelry to be purchased in any market. I remember sitting by the wife of a nobleman in a boat on the Neva who wore diamonds in her ears which, if they weighed one carat each, weighed fifteen. One solitaire on her finger was as large as a minie ball. In every other respect she presented a very modest and sweet appearance.

In the section between the new and old Capital there are few cities of any size, but the country is thickly populated and well improved. Cereals are grown to the height of cultivation, in spite of the crude agricultural machinery. The wheat in the great marts of Central Russia comes from this neck of country. Here one finds a few cottages on the farms. Some of the peasants own the land they cultivate. Wherever there is affluence in the rural districts there is a degree of improvement which evinces taste.

The better class of cottages resemble the Swiss *chalet*. There are broad balconies, and the eaves are decorated with woodwork, hand-carved. There is ornamentation around the windows, and the furniture is quite attractive.

Moscow is probably the most interesting city in all the Russias. Her palaces and treasuries are grand, and the features of her early days are maintained to the present time. There are the same walls about the Kremlin, and the battlements along the Volga, and traces of the prisons, which were constructed long before Napoleon took possession of the city in 1812.

There is little resemblance between the old and the new Capital, although they both contain nearly the same population. Moscow has about 650,000 inhabitants, while St. Petersburg contains almost 700,000. Moscow has been the central figure in all of Russia's history since her civilization. Here was the seat of the various wars, and from this city were issued the official mandates which have, from time to time, brought about not only revolutions, but peace and progress. The country to the north, east and south is gently undulating ; while to the west, whence flows the Volga, there are hills, forests and traces of early history. There is very little that is modern about the city. The hundreds and hundreds of domes on the cathedrals, churches and public institutions have the same highly-polished brass mountings that were seen in a less brilliant form generations ago. The thousands of chimes ring out the same melodies and national airs here that they rang during the time of Ivan the Terrible.

Hotels there are in abundance. The plan upon which one of them is kept is worthy of description. It is the Slavianski Bazaar, in the Kitai Gorod, or Chinese Town. It resembles both a summer and a winter garden. There are spacious reading-rooms, drinking-rooms and restaurants. The cuisine is conducted by French *chefs*. In the center of one of the largest dining-rooms is an immense fountain, and at its base a beautiful basin of running water, clear as crystal. In this there are always found a variety of fish, the favorite being the starlit, a species of carp, resembling in general appearance both the catfish and pike—an immense bull head, and a long, slender body, with a tough skin, but no scales. Americans and Englishmen generally order this fish. They go to the pool and select their members of the finny tribe darting about in the water. After the desired fish is indicated, a porter takes a small basket-net and captures it. Fifteen minutes later it is brought to you at your table, steaming, and covered with sauces and a compote of vegetables. The fish has ribs instead of fine bones, is pasty, and almost tasteless. It is not the deliciousness of the thing that induces one to make the order, but the novelty of it. There is an immense organ, which furnishes band music for the whole building, and one sees with the sweep of the eye men and women from almost every quarter of the globe. It is an interesting study, and you will never grow weary visiting the place. There are *diners du jour* served ; but Americans most enjoy a meal selected from the extensive *cartes*.

THE KREMLIN.

More difficulty is encountered in Moscow in the employment of *valets de place*—commissioners—than at any other city in the country, for there are very few people here who speak the English language, and comparatively few who speak French and German. I employed the only English-speaking courier to be procured, some time before leaving St. Petersburg, and he was constantly by my side.

Historically, the Kremlin is the center of attraction. Archæologists have failed to trace the name of the Kremlin, although it is supposed to be derived from the Russian word *kremen*, meaning an inclosed space. Originally, in 1367, it was surrounded by walls of oak. The foundation was of stone, and in the early days of the city it resisted the attacks of Tartars and other foes. It was burnt four centuries ago, and has since been rebuilt several times. It is about a mile and a half in circumference, and is entered by five gates, the principal of which is the *Spaski*, or the Redeemer's Gate, near the

Church of St. Basil, built in 1491. An immense tower was constructed two and a half centuries ago, and an English clockmaker placed in it a clock which gave time to the inhabitants for many years. The tower is of Gothic architecture.

Immediately over the Redeemer's Gate is a picture of the Saviour, which the natives hold in high veneration; and they always uncover their heads when they pass under it. For a long time a law was enforced which pu..ished with fifty prostrations or lashes all who did not uncover their heads when entering this gate. The stranger is always admonished to pay respect to the tradition, even to this day; and the swarms of people moving into and out of the Kremlin through this passageway are invariably bare-headed. During the early days, when criminals were executed in public, they were brought before this gate to offer their last prayers. This shrine, according to tradition, has saved Moscow many times from destruction by her enemies; and the natives hold that if it were destroyed all sorts of evil would come upon them. When Napoleon, in 1812, burned the Kremlin, the heat from the fire cracked the high walls surrounding it, and split the tower in the middle down as far as the picture; but not even the glass over nor the lamp suspended before it was injured. There is an inscription over the image to this effect: "Placed by the order of Alexander I."

During the latter part of the last century this vicinity was a refuge for thieves, murderers, tramps and scalawags, who at times terrorized the inhabitants.

Inside the Kremlin there are many places of interest. The Tower of Ivan the Terrible is worthy of the most attention. It was built in the seventeenth century, and consists of five stories, four of which are octangular, and the fifth cylindrical. It rises to a height of three hundred and twenty-five feet, and bears a cross of polished brass which glistens in the sunlight like gold. There are thirty-four bells of various sizes in the tower. The largest weighs sixty-four tons. Below is a chapel of magnificent proportions and splendid finishings. The famous bell of the Great Novgorod, known the world over as the Great Bell of Moscow, was at one time suspended in this tower. The ringing of the chimes on Easter day is a feature of the exercises commemorative of the occasion. Around the topmost point of the tower is a small space, where the traveler may pause and view the panorama of the city and surrounding country. There is surely nothing to surpass the grandeur of the scene in all of Europe.

The Bell of Moscow lies at the foot of this tower. Originally it weighed 36,000 pounds, and it required the services of more than a score of men to move the tongue. The bell was several times destroyed by fire, and once was broken when it fell to the ground. The first casting was in 1553. When it was recast in 1654 it weighed 288,000 pounds, its circumference was fifty-four and its thickness two feet. In 1706 it was again ruined by fire, and lay in fragments on the ground until the reign of Empress Anne, when it was last recast, in 1733. A fire four or five years afterward caused it to fall, and from its side a piece was broken, leaving a gap high and broad enough to admit of one walking into it upright. It is said that there were imperfections in the last casting, caused by jewels and other treasures being thrown into the liquid by the ladies of Moscow. At present it rests on a pedestal, and is said to weigh about a half million pounds. It is now twenty-six feet high and over sixty-seven feet in circumference, with a maximum thickness of two feet. In the summer months idlers are stretched out on its pedestal, sleeping, at almost any time of the day or night.

In the various chapels and churches located inside the Kremlin are sarcophagi, containing the remains of the early saints; dried drops of blood, claimed to be from the Saviour on the cross; alleged fragments of the cross itself; a spike, which it is held was used to nail the Saviour to the cross; paintings, and other sacred relics, before which worshipers fall upon their faces and supplicate. In a word, the Kremlin is a fortified museum of sacred things. Its contents at the present time are ancient treasures and relics. There are streams of people constantly pouring into it for worship and to satisfy curiosity; and here is concentrated the activity of the city. Idols are on every hand, and one is impressed with the memories of Greece, Jerusalem, Palestine, and everything that is related in Holy Writ.

The cathedrals in the great courts of the Kremlin contain more church valuables than could probably be found in all of the other cities in the country. The most precious mementoes of the early struggles of the Greek Church are stored within its walls; and it is regarded as a great privilege for natives to be permitted to worship here. They trudge, hungry, foot-sore and bleeding, thousands of miles for an opportunity to kiss the cross and drop their tears on these blood-stained floors.

The Treasury, containing most of the royal presents and treasures of the crown for centuries, is located hard by. It is an immense building, constructed less than a third of a century since, on the site of the ancient structure where lived many of the first rulers. Its design was a depository for venerated historical objects, and the hereditary jewels, wardrobes, carriages and equipages of those who helped to lay the foundations of the empire. Scores and scores of great rooms are filled with the wealth of the realm, stored away as mere keepsakes and objects of admiration. During the French invasion these treasures were taken to Niijni Novgorod, and thus escaped Napoleon's pillagers. Many relics similar to those in the Tower of London are here seen. There are beautiful old specimens of Russian armor, both for man and horse; weapons of every conceivable design and metal; and trophies taken from the countries conquered by Russia.

There are wagon-loads of the most valuable jewels, and tons of gold and silver. The court carriages fill a room as large as the most capacious town hall.

The principal church in the city—Church of Our Saviour—is without the walls of the Kremlin, and is surely the most magnificent in the world. It is said to have cost over forty million roubles. Its galleries of paintings, from the most celebrated artists, are excelled nowhere. A detailed description of it would occupy many pages in a book. The Tsars have, for centuries, been crowned in the Cathedral of the Assumption, which is the most sacred place, and consequently has the greatest interest for the natives, if not the strangers. There is more wealth in this church than can be found in any building in the United States outside the Treasury Department at Washington. Napoleon's men stabled their horses in the Cathedral of the Assumption, and committed all manner of sacrilegious acts in it. The floor is paved with jasper and agate, the gift of the Shah of Persia to the Tsar Alexis.

Russian churches as a whole are decorated internally in the highest order of art. In most of them the walls are almost entirely covered with pictures of the saints, the Virgin, and the Child. The Creator is generally represented by the figure of an old man, with long white hair and beard, giving it the triangle or symbol of the Trinity. Sometimes the Saviour is portrayed as sitting on the clouds, with one foot on the earth. In other instances He and the Virgin Mary are painted one on either side. Around the brows of the saints are halos of glory in silver-gilt; sometimes it is in pure gold, set with pearls and other precious stones. The Virgin Mary is occasionally dressed in gold or silver-gilt, from which covering the face and hands are visible out of the mass of rich settings.

Some of these portraits are very ancient, and are intrinsically extremely valuable. Most of them are blackened by time, and at a glance appear as dark spaces with bright surroundings. The artists were unable to give the Virgin a graceful form or attractive features.

The Greek is the Church of Russia, and it is maintained at the expense of the Government. The religion is almost a part of the laws, and is enforced upon all subjects of the crown. There is a church officer in the Privy Council—the Cabinet—who administers the laws. Everybody is supposed to belong to the church and to contribute to its support. There is a close alliance between the laws of the church and those of the Government. The proceeds from each are interchangeable.

There is a museum in Moscow worthy of prolonged visits, and a zoological garden, and picture galleries, of much interest. The Riding School is the most celebrated in the world. The building has the largest room unsupported by pillar or prop to be found in the universe. It is nearly six hundred feet in length, about one hundred and sixty-five feet in breadth and forty-two feet in height. Internally it is ornamented with *bas reliefs* of men in armor and ancient trophies. There are twenty stoves for heating purposes, and they are all made of white earthenware, rising to the ceiling. Small windows, high above the ground, afford light and ventilation. The long, low building looks somber, and besides being used as a place of amusement for the populace, is a training-school for cavalrymen. Two regiments have ample room for evolutions and manœuvres, and the entertainments given by civilians and the military in this vast building take high rank.

CHAPTER XVI

Officers are nowhere so officious as in Moscow.

One morning, after visiting the Treasury and various p o i n t s within the walls of the Kremlin, I sat down on a step leading to the entrance of a building to await the return of the guide, who had gone somewhere for the purpose of bribing an official to obtain admission to one of the private rooms of the palace. The guard hastened up, roared out some Russian words, and motioned me to move on.

I didn't move, but sat and looked the fellow in the face, as stoically as an ordinary Indian. I was in no one's way. The step I sat upon was clearly outside the range of pedestrians, and no possible harm could come if I sat there a whole month of thirty-one days. But I finally moved.

A minute after I refused to amble to the order of the official connected with the building a soldier, on his regular patrol, came up. He motioned for me to move. At first I pretended not to understand. Then he grew red in the face and warm under the collar; walked up, took me by the arm and gave me a start.

Fifty paces further on I stopped, leaned up against a window-sill, far away from anyone, and proceeded to wait for my courier. The soldier brought his gun to a present and marched toward me. When a dozen feet from me he made a motion with his whole facial features and arm at the same time, which said if I didn't get outside the square I would get into prison. Remembering Siberia, the Fort-

ress up the river at St. Petersburg, the many dungeons with their tor-
tures, and lastly the inclosure where the rifle speaks the execution, I
moved out—clear outside the Kremlin and into the street.

"No one is permitted to linger around here after he comes out of
a building. He must move on. The authorities are afraid of Nihilists, and suspect every one who pauses about the Kremlin," said the
courier. "Had you persisted in refusing to go outside, you would
have been arrested and sent to prison. If it could have been shown
that you *might* have designs against any of the institutions of the empire, you would never have been heard of."

While I was standing in the street awaiting the courier, who succeeded by the persuasive influence of a rouble in securing admission
to a forbidden place, an undertaker passed me. He moved in the
center of the street, and on his head carried a great Russia-iron coffin
ornamented with sham silver and decorated with a huge floral offer-
ing. The flowers were of wax. A small boy followed the undertaker and carried a soldering apparatus. The corpse is placed in the
coffin and hermetically sealed in. The funeral procession is frequently led by the corpse in a coffin on the head of one man.

There are probably five hundred places in Moscow alone where
shrines are sold. One goes into shops and stores of every description
and finds a supply of these articles. A drug, book, clothing or hardware
store will have a stock of shrines. The landlord at your hotel keeps
a few on hand for guests too hurried in their departure to allow them
to be particular in purchasing.

All shrines are made of brass, and one can get them anywhere
from the size of the hand up to eight by ten feet. Most of them have
a painting, a chromo, or other colored picture of the head of the
Saviour or the Virgin Mary, in the center; and usually about the
picture are sprays in the brass, like rays of the sun. Many have arrangements for a candle or a lamp immediately above or below the
painting. The shrine shops are a perfect glitter of brass.

Going through the streets in any city or village one sees a shrine
at least every two hundred feet, and the natives are kept in a perfect
ferment of bowing and crossing. Every bridge, even if it be but a
dozen steps in length, has from one to six shrines. The long bridges
at St. Petersburg, Moscow and Niijni Novgorod have shrine-houses,
with a lot of candles burning, an attendant, and arrangements for worship. All these shrines are maintained, directly or indirectly, by the
empire. As the churches are supported from the public funds, it

makes little difference whether the money comes directly from the treasury or from the coffers of the church.

Four horses are driven to the street cars in Moscow. As at St. Petersburg, Paris, London and many other European cities, the cars are two-storied, and the upper part is open, with long seats, and is reached by a winding stairway at the rear. But the cars here are very long. Below and above almost a hundred passengers may sit. There are a conductor, a driver and a hostler. The latter rides the foremost "off" horse. The driver rings a bell almost continually. The conductor gives a check to each passenger, who must pay twenty copecks a ride ; and the speed is about that of street cars in America.

Shops and stores of all kinds do not open in Russia till nine o'clock in the morning, unless there is some special thing in view ; and they close at five in the afternoon. The jewelry shops have a display in the windows ; but when one enters he sees no goods. The keeper jumps to his feet, and, when you call for what you want, he begins to open drawers and take out trays. Only dry-goods shops make a full display, and these do so very bunglingly.

Government buildings are all painted a dirty light yellow. The paint is a kind of wash, and is put on with a broad brush attached to a pole.

As a general thing the hotels are as good as the traveler encounters in the far western and southern portions of the United States. But he gets more fleas and other vermin here than in America. Salt meats, fish and insipid vegetables form the principal diet. Caviar— the eggs of salmon, sturgeon and some of the other large fish, salted or cured in oil and pressed—is seen everywhere in a dining-room. It is generally eaten as a relish, like pickles. In the markets great hogsheads full of caviar, and cakes of it as large as tubs, are visible on every hand, and on them are paddles, so that customers may help themselves. Some Americans learn to relish the stuff, but they are few. It is sold in cans in every American city. A friend of mine in Washington had some in his house one day when Auntie, the new cook, entered, carrying a can at arm's length. "Wat dis yeah stuff, master?" she inquired ; and upon being informed said, "Well, it certainly do hab a werry lonesome smell." She was right. Russians say it is a stomach-stayer, and will help to prevent seasickness.

After dinner lighted candles are placed on the table, and nearly everybody smokes. The women are inveterate smokers.

The natives are slovenly and ignorant, live on black bread and a vegetable soup that is awful, and drink strong tea and vodka like water. The soup is a curiosity. It has a large proportion of cabbage and meat, beet-root, sausage and vinegar; sometimes varenookla, corn brandy boiled with fruit and spice; and kostia, boiled rice and plums.

Invariably when Moscovan friends meet they kiss twice, once on either cheek. The men greet each other in this way, the same as women. Frequently I have seen great, burly men here, with flowing beards, smoking strong cigars, meet and kiss each other so affectionately that their lips gave out sounds like the suction-valves in air-pumps. Sometimes they forget to take their pipes or cigars from their mouths, and the collisions are amusing to the spectator.

A Russian never thinks of announcing himself at the door. He enters without knocking; and if he discovers the occupant of the room is not looking for him and does not desire his presence, he simply sits down and waits, as if he expected to be lifted up by the shoulders and heaved out.

I have never seen a lightning-rod in all the country. This is not because there is no lightning here, but because the people do not believe in rods to conduct to the ground the deadly bolts. They believe it would be trifling with the Inevitable and defying the Invisible. I believe Ajax came from another part of the globe than this.

Nearly all the chimneys at the factories, and many of those on residences, have sieve-like coverings, to prevent sparks and cinders from flying out.

For some unaccountable reason a charge is attached for passport examination amounting to one rouble and thirty copecks here, while at other places the charges are less than one-fourth this sum. When one enters Russia he gets his passport *vised* by the local officer where he stops, and is permitted to remain in the country on this six months. If he stays over this time without a new passport and a renewed permission he is fined thirty copecks a day. He must take out at the expiration of his six months, if he has not a new passport, a Russian *address-billet*. The usual fee for examining a passport is thirty copecks, and it must be examined at every city, village and station where the traveler stops. The same routine is necessary everywhere; and when one leaves the country he is stopped on the frontier, his passport examined, and he must get permission to depart. But all this is no worse than the fee of five dollars charged by the State Department at Washington for a passport, simply certifying that the bearer is a citizen of the United States.

Visitors to Moscow almost invariably run over to Niijni Novgorod, where the National Fair is held every year, beginning about the first of August and lasting till the weather becomes extremely cold. Niijni Novgorod has about 50,000 population, is the chief town of the province of the same name, and is an interesting place to visit. It is situated at the confluence of the Volga and Oka rivers, and is an important shipping point. Boats land here from distances of over 2,000 miles. Niijni is thirteen hours by express from Moscow, directly west, and the railroad tariff is twenty-four roubles. The hotel accommodations are pleasant, if one does not get caught in the crowd.

. The celebrated fair of Niijni Novgorod is but a mart for wares produced by the inhabitants of the city and surrounding country. The fair spreads out like an immense town of shops on the triangular point of land between the Oka and the Volga, which can be traced for many miles, with its steamers, like so many straws, floating down to the Caspian, fourteen hundred miles beyond. The scenery is beautiful. The forest of masts looks like a floating town, and covers the surface of the Oka almost completely. There is every conceivable shape of ships : the quaint barques and schooners, coming as they do from the most distant parts of the empire, with peculiar cargoes, in charge of ragged Tartars, Cossacks, Greeks and Turks.

This fair is a succession of bazaars and booths, where men, women and children sell their products. About that portion of the city where the fair is held is a constant stream of carts, in long strings ; crowds of traders with great beards and fierce manners ; vendors of liquid refreshments and white rabbit-skins ; greasy monks collecting copecks from those who fear to withhold their charity, lest their transactions be influenced by the Evil Spirit. There are beggars here and thieves innumerable. But it is worth the trip to see the sights.

I have almost confined myself in describing the institutions and customs of Russia to the three or four larger cities and the country about them, for the reason that the most interesting features are here to be found. What one learns in the sections I devote myself to in these notes gives him a very good idea of what he will see in a trip through all the civilized country.

CHAPTER XVII.

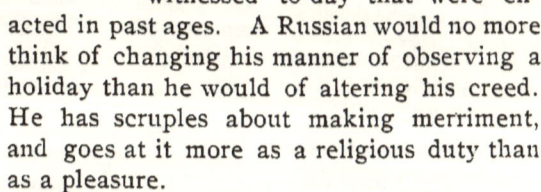

Very different from those in any other part of the world are the holidays in Russia. While in the United States and most of the countries of Europe the festivities have changed with the character of the people and the surroundings, in the empire of Alexander the same scenes are to be witnessed to-day that were enacted in past ages. A Russian would no more think of changing his manner of observing a holiday than he would of altering his creed. He has scruples about making merriment, and goes at it more as a religious duty than as a pleasure.

For several days before the coming of Christmas the villages and cities are busy places. Elaborate decorations are always made. Rows of colored lights are put up around residences, along the streets, and in the promenades and gardens. These are fed by little pots of grease and are tastefully arranged. High walls, miles in length, and fantastically decorated with colored lights, are sometimes erected. Calcium lights are hung on the sidewalks, buildings and hills surrounding the villages and cities. Ice palaces are constructed, brilliantly illuminated, and in them fairs are held till the new year is ushered in.

The day before Christmas the people hang out decorations, consisting of flags, bunting, rags, carpets, cloths and highly-colored garments. Whole sides of large buildings along the principal thoroughfares are covered with these. They simply hang from the windows, and the effect upon a stranger is most bewildering. When the wind blows, the snow flies and the decorations flutter the scene cannot be described. When midnight comes the bells ring, guns are fired and the serenaders start upon their rounds.

Stringed instruments and bass drums are used. The Russians sing beautifully, and the music they produce is charming. The rich, deep bass voices harmonize perfectly with the clear, sweet and high tenors. Sometimes the voices of the monks join in, for these have no hesitancy in making a night of it on such an occasion. The serenaders do not cease their music till it is time for Mass in the churches, when they wend their way churchward, and depositing their instruments on the sidewalks, fall upon their knees, bump their heads upon the pavement in front of the churches, cross themselves repeatedly, and say their prayers. I have seen them keep up this exercise for a full half hour, till it seemed impossible for them to either find the strength to continue it or keep from freezing.

Inside the church there are few people, the worship being conducted by each individual on the sidewalk. But if you open the great door of oak, iron or filagree work, a strange scene can be witnessed. The floor is of marble or tiling. Above the iconastas, or altar, is an icon—a picture of Christ, or the Madonna, in oil, and framed in gold. Before it is a grease lamp, burning dimly. At one side of the room stand a dozen or more monks, in long robes, chanting service. At times the music varies, taking in short but charming anthems, peculiar Russian compositions; yet it does not cease for hours. A priest is walking about the auditorium, carrying an incense-burner, which smokes to the verge of suffocation. He murmurs in indistinct terms the service, swinging the censer first up and down before the icon over the iconastas, and then before all the images and pictures in the great room. These performances he repeats a number of times, the music of the voices continuing without any accompaniment, as musical instruments are not permitted in the Greek Church or its monasteries.

While these services are being conducted inside the church an occasional man or woman enters, and proceeding before the iconastas falls upon his or her face and moans piteously, at times frothing at the mouth and beating the floor furiously. The scene reminds one of a Free Methodist meeting, where the congregation get "the power." The priest swings his censer over the prostrate form "till the devil is frightened away." This in no way interferes with the singing, and only momentarily interrupts the ceremony of the priest incensing the images. The expression on the faces of the penitents is excrutiating. The services are in the Slav language. The priests are in splendid robes of brocade.

The shrines are pieces of solid silver or gold, weighing a quarter of a ton, while the diamonds, rubies and other precious stones around the icons in the finer churches at St. Petersburg and Moscow are worth fortunes. Incense burns at every turn from diminutive blood-red glass cups. They are never permitted to die out. Regular sermons are not preached, as there is but one sermon a year in these churches.

All Russian churches stand due east or west, with the altar east. The object is to meet the sun in every turn, the sun being the light of God. After the services at the churches the people return to their homes to feast, and then go out into the streets to celebrate. The church requires a great deal of fasting previous to this period, and as a consequence the people are in condition for an unusual amount of gormandizing. The Russians fast seven weeks in Lent, three weeks in June, and from November till Christmas; and they have so many holidays that only one hundred and thirty working days remain for them in the year.

Kostia—boiled rice and plums—is the only thing partaken of on Christmas Eve. Next day, however, the people begin by eating bountifully of borsch—a soup made of meat, sausages, beet-root, cabbage and vinegar. Cabbage in every form is served, and vodka is drunk copiously. Then follow quantities of caviar, dried and frozen fish, pickles and sweets.

The calendar in Russia is eleven days behind that in America; but if the people are a little late in getting started in their holiday festivities they make up for the loss of time by their vigor. Among the amusements they enjoy are the ice-hill and races. Skating is also popular. The ice-hill is somewhat similar to the toboggan of America. A framework, with steps up one side, is erected. On the upper part is a small stage, covered with an ornamental roof supported by four pillars, and a steep inclined plane on the other side, which terminates in a long run. Water is poured upon this, and after freezing, which is instantaneous, the slide is perfect.

At one time a custom prevailed of going about from one friend's house to another, masked, and committing every conceivable prank. Then the people feasted on blinnies—a pancake similar to the English crumpet. Those who do not go to the ice-hills or rivers to slide or skate participate in the carnival or races. The spirit of children seems to prevail in the formation of the carnival, as men and women mask and ride hobby-horses through the streets, blowing horns, beating drums and playing the rag-tag.

The holidays are not alone celebrated by the elder persons. The children have their sports. As soon as they appear on the streets in the morning they begin to pelt each other with rice, beans, bonbons and preserved fruits. It is a kind of free treat, in which the parents frequently indulge and make up what takes the form of Christmas trees in America. The children form in groups and march through

the streets and from house to house, singing carols, and are given
sweets wherever they go.   They are a happy lot, even though they
have not the advantages the children of many other countries enjoy.

At night there are grand balls at the halls and mansions of the
nobility.   These are very gay affairs; and when at the private residences there are the most sumptuous repasts, the higher grades of
wine flowing freely.   The Russians are the most liberal in their entertainments of any people in the world.   Dinners are often spread at
private houses which cost three hundred rou-
bles a plate.   The *menu* is the finest that French
caterers can produce, and the cards and favors
are of gold and diamonds.   Before Nihilism became so common members of the royal family
attended the Christmas
fetes when they ventured
at no other pub-
lic places.   Now

the officers of the army and navy are the most distinguished guests.
The guests always sit down at table when supper or lunch is served,
but the host and hostess never do.   They walk around, chatting with
the company, drinking their health, and seeing that the greatest
amount of wine is consumed and the utmost levity possible is aroused.
The ladies' toilets are the most superb in the world, but would perhaps be considered flashy in the United States.

There are extra illuminations in the grounds surrounding the residences of the nobility where these balls and banquets are held. Besides the walls of colored lights, lamps of variegated shades are set in the snow, making them look like fairy lights. When the gray of dawn begins to appear after Christmas the merry dancers cease their rounds. More wine is brought, and vodka is served. Then tea makes its appearance in samovars. Men and women drink and smoke till the sun appears. These festivities continue till after the New Year. The people dress in bright costumes, and business is almost entirely suspended. It is considered sacrilegious to let such worldly affairs as commercial transactions interfere with holiday festivities.

But the really great holidays in Russia are at Easter-time. If you were in Moscow at midnight when Easter came in and were not prepared for what you saw and heard, you would conclude that the millennium had come. Each of the five hundred and twenty-five church domes has a chime of bells. Sometimes as many as thirty or forty bells are found in one set of chimes. Each dome will average at least ten bells, so that there must be over five thousand altogether. These bells are all of the heaviest bronze, and being hung far apart harmonize beautifully and sound differently from the chimes in any other place in the world. The very instant the midnight hour arrives every one of these bells, and all the hand-bells in the city, are rung with vigor and for hours. The inhabitants rush from their homes and the hotels and run through the streets, crying : "He is risen!" Men kiss each other, and women engage in the most promiscuous osculations. The priests and monks form in procession, and, marching through the streets, chant the services of the church. Sometimes they proceed to the Volga, and wading into the water waist-deep, bless it and pray to the stars. The people gather in the Kremlin, and during the exercises every one goes bare-headed, under penalty of corporeal punishment. The scene is impressive and would have a decided effect on the stranger but for the knowledge that the most devout celebrant may be caught stealing his handkerchief on the morrow.

CHAPTER XVIII.

In no feature of Russian life is there a wider variance between the order of things in America than in courtship and marriage.

Everything is done by negotiation, and marriage ambassadors are quite as common and respectable as probate lawyers in the United States.

Until a few years ago the popular age for marriage was very low. Boys fourteen or fifteen years old and girls from twelve to fourteen married ; and the parents were universally glad of it. As soon as the girl got out of her swaddling clothes, or the boy could amble around on the streets, the parents began to cast about for a match. When an opportunity presented itself the ambassador was employed and negotiations were begun. Thus it frequently happened that there was a betrothal before either of the contracting parties knew anything about the existence or object of the marriage vow. Finally this thing was carried too far, and the Government declared it a crime for persons to marry under or above certain ages. Now the male cannot marry under eighteen or over eighty years of age, and the females are forbidden to wed till they are sixteen or after they become sixty. And there are restraints against frequent marriages which would quite discourage the professional widowers and widows of the United States. If you marry twice the law of the church, which is the law of the land, gives you two years' penance, which means exclusion for that length of time from holy communion. Should you marry three times, five years' penance is given. To marry a fourth time is to sever relations from the church forever and invite the condemnation of the Saviour. Remarriages are unknown, and separations are final.

Girls of marriageable age and women of respectability are very seldom seen upon the streets alone. Generally a male servant follows in close proximity. Should a boy or man see a girl or woman he admires, he makes post-haste to an ambassador, employs him, and marriage negotiations begin. It is the business of the negotiator to represent to the parents and the girl the good qualities of the young man ; to show his ability, his grace, fine appearance and business worth to

their best advantage.   He generally pleads his case well.   Seldom is
time given for consideration.   If the lineage and the personal qualities suit the parents first, and the girl latterly, the offer is accepted.
It is then the business of the ambassador to fetch the young man.
The couple kiss, fix the date, and partake of a betrothal supper, the
only persons present being the family of the young lady, the young
man and his negotiator.   No announcement of the match is made.

Not until the wedding knot is tied does the glib ambassador get
his pay.   It then depends upon the station of the parties to the
match, the difficulty and intricacy of the case and the liberality of
the client.   Sometimes both parties make him presents and he fares
well.   Usually he profits to about the same extent as the prosecuting
lawyer in the United States when he gets a divorce proceeding
through.

At one time there was a fixed day for match-making.   It was
Whitsun-Monday, and was known as the "day for choosing brides."
The summer gardens were the exhibiting places.   The anxious
mothers were present in force, and the solicitous fathers looked after
their sons.   The girls were dressed in all the finery they could buy or
borrow.   They had silks, satins, laces and jewels.   Some of them
were gaudy.   The girls were placed in lines, and the fathers with
their sons passed along in review.   The latter made mental memo-
randa of the girls, and during the following week negotiations were
begun.   Although this custom has been almost abolished, it is yet observed to some extent ; and the summer garden on Whitsun-Monday
is an interesting place to visit.   The girls are modest and ofttimes
pretty.

Russian marriages invariably take place at night ; and if they are
among the peasants, to which class the negotiation custom is now
mostly confined, the ambassador who made the match is the principal
guest.   First, the wedding garments receive the priest's blessing, the
parents solemnly bless the daughter and son at their respective homes,
and the sacred pictures are three times waved over the heads of the
contracting parties.   If the couple are of sufficient importance to
have attendants, the lady of honor leads the bride-elect to the carriage, and then they proceed to the church.   The bridegroom in pros-
pect is meanwhile at his own home, and couriers from his affianced
bride's abode run to tell him it is time to meet her at the sanctuary.
So the bridegroom-elect puts out for the church.

When the pair proceed to the altar they carry wax tapers ; and
the belief is that the taper which first burns out marks the one first

to die.   In the upper circles there are the wedding ring and the ceremony pledging faith and fealty, much the same as in America.   While
the latter part of the ceremony is taking place mixed wine and water
is passed to the assembly.   After the ceremony the priest and bridal
party walk three times around the maloy, where rest the cross and
Gospels.   When the exhortation is said the pair must kiss three times.
Then there is a benediction, and the bride and bridegroom go together and kiss all the holy pictures on the iconastas.   The whole
proceeding occupies half an hour.

If the marriage is in society circles a feast follows at the house
of the bride's parents, and the guests get drunk.   If the marriage is
in the families of the peasantry the bridegroom leads the bride to his
home.   There, on the steps to the house, his parents stand to greet
them, and they are blessed with bread and salt.   While this is going
on some of the neighbors present give them milk to drink and pour
over them barley and down.   The first is in hope that the children of
the couple may be white instead of black, and the second that the
newly-mated may live harmoniously, for many Russian husbands and
wives fight like dogs and cats.

The couple enter the house and receive the customary courtesies
and favors.   They sit down on a bench, and the mother-in-law or
some other female relative removes the handkerchief which covers
the blushing bride's face, braids her loose tresses and places upon her
head a married woman's head-dress.

It is now late at night, may be, but a wedding breakfast is served
with great spirit.   Originally it was the custom, among the peasants,
for the bride and bridegroom to retire during the breakfast.   Then,
as now, all men on all occasions wore boots, and although then, as
now, every bed chamber had a bootjack, the bride must pull off her
lord's boots.   Before the marriage ceremony he fixed a scheme to de-
termine her lot in life.   In one boot he secreted the surplus gold and
silver coin he possessed.   If the bride pulled the boot containing the
valuables first she not only got the money, but immunity against ever
drawing her husband's boots in the future.   If, however, she first got
hold of the boot not containing the money, she was subject to her
husband's whims.   If he chose to use her hands for a bootjack at any
time he was licensed to do so, and she had no recourse.   Some such
plan as this in America might settle the question : Who shall get up
first and kindle the fire ?

Of course, in the higher Russian circles, the customs partake
more of the American and English.   But in the country and among

inary folks the olden-time usages are observed even now. ife is expected to stay at home and look after her many children and know nothing. The fasts and festivals of the church afford ut the only relief from monotony a Russian wife ever finds. Living away from the world, it is no wonder the Russian women so often depend upon the witchcraft of female medical advisers for their physical cures and have so many superstitions about spiritual ailments. All Russian women are superstitious, and the percentage of those educated is probably lower than among any other civilized women in the world.

CHAPTER XIX.

There are the strangest superstitions sur
and directing the conduct of funerals in Ru

A native never thinks of passing a funer
going through the streets without uncovering h.
of a coffin is sufficient to quell a quarrel, while a h
stopped at the appearance of a funeral *cortege*.

Every undertaker is supplied with a number of torch
poles, the shape of a street lamp-post. These are carried at th
of funeral processions. Generally six of these torches or lamps
at the head of a procession; but occasionally a dying man or woma.
may request that twenty, forty, or some larger number of lights be carried, and then it is a torchlight procession.

The monks of the Church of Russia have charge of the funeral
arrangements, and in the absence of friends they do the mourning
and moaning. Pitiable scenes, in the eyes of strangers, are often
presented by the monks, who make no regular charge for their services, but expect from two roubles upward.

After the services at the house the monks form the procession to
the grave. The corpse is swathed in a gown which sometimes presents a flashy appearance, and jewels are strewn over its front.
When the coffin is ready to be lowered into the grave a perfect howl
is set up by the monks; but they are hushed by the one in charge of
the ceremony. Then begin the tossing of dirt into the depths and
the chanting of the death-song. When the corpse is in the ground,
the grave filled, and the procession starts upon its return to the dis-
tressed home, there are smiles and hearty greetings. At the house
there is a feast and a flow of wine, to which all who attend the funeral sit down.

Coffins and caskets in Russia are seldom made of anything other
than metal. One of the leading undertakers in St. Petersburg told
me that only the paupers were buried in wooden coffins. The wealthy,
he explained, always order the "finished" iron or tin. This, I was
shown, meant gilt on Russia iron or the ordinary tin-plate. Some

the very minute of the demise, the age of the deceased, the disease from which he or she died, and any other information of interest. They present a lugubrious appearance with their long black robes, high white collars, cocked hats with black plumes, drum-major staffs, great cords and sashes hanging almost to the ground, and their funereal gait. Everything is in charge of these

Holland Announcing a death.

Naples

Funeral of a Child.

three men. The family of the deceased have no care in the preparations. The keys of the house are carried by the trio of managers. The family make out a list of friends who are to be given special notice of the death, and there their physical labor ends. Unless specially desired to the contrary, the body is clothed without interference or suggestion from the family. At the funeral these three men ride at the head of the procession, and in the absence of a minister perform the last sad rites. At Naples I saw a funeral procession. It was a fashionable one, and was in charge of four priests. When it moved from the house of the deceased the priests sat at the corners of the coffin, inside the hearse. They looked sad, and moaned in heart-rending tones. There were four horses to the hearse, and they were completely covered with black cloth. The front door to the house of the deceased was also covered with black cloth. As soon as the ceremonies were completed at the grave the procession started back to the house. The black high hats of the priests were removed, but they occupied the hearse, and the door to it was closed, although the temperature was 112° in the shade. Instead of tears, now there were smiles and roars of laughter. Three of them were eating as the horses ran through the streets, while the fourth priest smoked. The intention was to relieve the family of the pain of the death. Sometimes when a small child dies at Naples six Sisters carry the coffin and walk at the head of the procession. Occasionally the whole procession is on foot. In front of the coffin are two small boys, one carrying a cross, the other a basket of flowers. A priest and a small boy may also be seen in the front at times. Both are in church-robes. The Italians make a funeral very impressive in some respects.

There is a little village in the South of France where funeral services are carried out in an exceedingly strange manner. The person who chances to be at the bedside when the deceased breathes his last may say the first rite. This consists principally of a description of the appearance of the dead at the last moment in life, a repetition of the final words, and a detailed statement of the treatment the deceased received at the last hour. It is presumed that all present at the funeral want to know whether the departed friend was prepared to cross the river. Then each member of the immediate family is called upon to relate reminiscences of the deceased.

Anecdotes affecting his or her past life and illustrating good qualities are proper, and the opportunity is invariably accepted. Then there is an obituary essayist. He tells of the life of the deceased in a connected form. If the ceremony is over an infant this officer at the funeral delineates what the deceased might have been had it lived. The funeral *cortege* is on foot, and the coffin is carried on the back of a donkey—a sacred animal. At the grave there is little mourning, but much ceremony.

Here the minister presides, and the teachings of the Bible are

On a hill to the east of Moscow stands an old prison. From this point depart for exile in Siberia all of the condemned enemies of the empire who are convicted in this locality.

There are no scenes presented on the stage affecting or thrill-ose depicting of exiles

Every
they
from their
open court
walls, where
permitted to
eir relatives and
ewell. The proceed-
gs are more agonizing
iberia is a living death,
inister to their spiritual
t will palliate the physical

pires and domes of Moscow as
rld adieu, as did the condemned
Sighs from the Doge's Palace at
for execution a century ago. About
die on the way to Siberia. Many re-

enunciated by oral illustration ~ts held open, and the extinctness up on the lid, the eyes are ~ut. Whenever the grief-stricken fam- of life impressed upon thos~ coffin is opened, the corpse laid

ily bursts
out in ago-
nizing tears
it is inform-
ed that a sin
i s b e i n g
committed
by this in-
terference.
The work
of the fune-
ral day be-
gins in the early morning and seldom ends before nightfall. Then
there is an assembly at the late
home of the deceased, and the
culinary ability of the family is
tested. Good wines flow, philosophy on death and the life beyond
is preach-
e d ; a n d
when all are
dismissed a
very good
f r a m e of
mind pre-
vails. A
guard is
kept over
the grave
f o r thirty
days. A su-
perstition
prevails

A funeral in the Alps.

that the spirit of the dead, being dissatisfied with the life eternal, may
return and take away the mortal body.

In the Alps of Switzerland one morning I met a couple of old

fuse to sleep or eat, wishing to wear their lives away; and some succeed before reaching their destination.

On the road to exile the prisoners are frequently visited by the peasants, who sympathize with them, serve to them delicacies and offer words of cheer. It has become a custom of late for the officers in charge, in order to avoid the jeers of the crowds and harrowing scenes when relatives meet, to pass through the thickly-settled communities at night. Mothers, wives and sweethearts often follow the exiles for days and weeks, until the border-line is passed, when the last parting takes place.

If there are many of the exiles when the start is made to Siberia they are frequently taken all the distance on foot. Should the party be of small size, it is customary to extend some conveniences. Prisoners who can afford to leave civilization in comparative luxury depart in tarantasses—covered hacks or voitures—a comfortable vehicle of transportation. There are always a certain number of days given the exile who provides his own transportation within which to reach the boundary-line and enter the exile kingdom. A date is fixed for departure and also the time when he must report to the officers at the last outpost. The intervening time is occasionally spent in an enjoyable way with the officers having charge of the exile, who live in luxurious fashion at inns and about the communes *en route*.

One cannot imagine a journey more gloomy and exhausting than that upon which an average party of exiles starts from Moscow, not to mention the sadness which must occupy the reflections of the prisoners. They journey ten or twelve miles a day when on foot, and are afforded regular sleeping-places. Each carries a chain weighing four pounds upon his feet and hands. Murderers, patriots, conspirators and thieves, men and women, are chained together without distinction.

Up to a few years ago more than sixty thousand exiles to Siberia passed through Kazan every year; but the authorities say the number has been reduced two-thirds at the present time. The exiles are permitted to communicate with each other on their journey; and after each has related his or her experience to the other, explaining the circumstances under which apprehension, conviction and sentence were brought about, they try to make one another as happy as possible, the cheerful ones singing songs, while the sad ones wail in chorus.

Over the Ural Mountains, beyond the confines of Europe, the

exiles plod their way, crossing rivers, wading through mud, climbing hills, in rain or snow; descending into the region of Zabaikalia, beyond Lake Baikal to the River Kara, and probably by water to the end of their journey. On the way are several houses of detention, where the common criminals are confined; one is for political convicts of the delicate sex. These prisons are detached buildings on the river's bank, and at intervals of from five to eight miles. They are under the general supervision of a chief. The political prison, consisting of four buildings, has a specific organization and a special management. A short distance above Oust-Kara is what is known as the Lower Kara Prison. Then the High Kara Prison is reached, and further on the Amour, a prison named after the River Amour.

Political prisons are recognized by the characteristic surroundings. Those destined for ordinary convicts have outer walls or palisades on the three sides, the fourth being open, with the front windows facing the public thoroughfare. The political prisons are built in the middle of a court, and are surrounded on every side by walls so high that you can only see the roof; so that the outside world is shut off almost as completely as if the prisoner was within the confines of his ultimate destination. Much more freedom is given the common criminal than is granted the political offender.

The last pull at the heart-strings of the exiles and the friends who follow them is on the frontier-line. Posts at frequent intervals mark the line between Siberia and Russia proper. There is a patrol of soldiers and detectives on this frontier who do not permit anyone to enter into or emerge from it unless by special permission of the Governor-General. If the incoming exiles arrive on the frontier-line early in the day, and many friends have followed, frequently two or three hours are given for the parting. This is the point where the tear-fountains are pumped dry. Fathers part with wives and children forever. Mothers press to their bosoms sons and daughters for the last time on earth. Here the friends turn back to their homes on the long, dreary route, over which they have traveled for weeks, and the condemned disappear in the prison-land.

So much has been written about life in exile that I shall pass over this with very brief mention.

Siberia is like one great barrack. It is a territory, too arid and barren for successful utility, but in many places is covered with fine forests and dotted with valuable mines. It is generally believed, outside of Russia, that all Siberian exiles are required to work in the mines. This is not true. Only a portion are sentenced to the mines—those who are condemned to hard labor. Exile in Siberia means, as a general rule, only enforced life in a certain expanse of country. The Government allows a pension to some exiles sufficient to scantily clothe and feed them. The allowance is about six roubles a month. This will procure a place to sleep and coarse food. Once here, it is next to impossible to get away. The exile in the first place is landed

in the heart of a wild country, surrounded by little or no civilization, and, being clothed in uniform, it is out of the question to think of escape, even though he is provided with food and raiment for the long journey.

Much like sections of Alaska and the extreme northwestern portion of the United States is the face of the country in Siberia. There are settlements, villages formed by exiles and soldiers, and in some instances small manufactories. But the officers in the Russian army, who have control of everything, make the existence of the inhabitants miserable where the exiles themselves would secure a little sunshine. There are a few cases on record where the exiles, by dint of much labor and shrewd management, have succeeded in accumulating some property and have used this to effect escape ; but they are strokes of fortune rare as strokes of lightning, and are not worth the struggle.

Once in Siberia the exile is the same as in jail, with the exception that he has the open air and plenty of room in which to move. Inasmuch as no firearms, except those in the possession of the soldiers, are allowed in the country, and the colonies are kept small, a successful rising is not possible. If the exiles were permitted to commingle freely, and were afforded an opportunity to organize, even without arms, they would make frequent trouble, for they are in a desperate frame of mind. In the first place, the majority of the exiles are persons who have offended the throne, and they were moved to the offense through a desire to check real or fancied wrongs against the people. They were frenzied by despotism. People of this character have no regard for life and no fear of death. The Nihilist who destroyed Alexander II. was willing to be destroyed at the same time. All who have moved against a royal life in Russia have been willing to die for their acts.

Quite as many or more army and other officers are stationed in Siberia to guard the exiles, who number possibly hundreds of thousands, as are in the military and naval services of the United States. So extreme have been the punishments of the exiles, and so unjust, and so many innocent persons have been exiled, that many of the Government's officers are becoming disgusted, and a number of them are ready to conspire with the men over whom they are expected to keep guard. Should Russia become engaged in a war which would lessen the Siberian forces sufficiently to warrant an insurrection, it would surely come, and the system of exile would be no more. It is maintained, because it is a dreadful mode of punishment and enables the Government to drag-net many of its subjects and suppress all open dissatisfaction at a comparatively small expense. It would require an enormous outlay to provide prisons for the exiles. As it is they are dumped into a country which they cannot leave, where they are safe, and are given a trifling pittance to subsist upon.

American and English excursionists sometimes extend their trips to Southern Siberia and have a pleasant journey. Here the climate is very like that in Finland and Old Russia. Towns, small cities and beautiful residences are seen. In places there is active life, and enterprise hardly to be expected under the circumstances. Other portions of Siberia would be developed were it not that they cannot be made either pleasant or profitable places of abode with so many criminals and eccentric persons.

Among the most numerous class in Siberia are the writers. They are very readily convicted and summarily dealt with. Landed in Siberia, it is the ambition of the educator of public opinion to tell the outside world his condition and the horrors of the country. Here one could find sufficient foundation for any number of romances and heroic narratives. There are no mails, but various schemes are resorted to in order to get letters out to friends. Occasionally, in the columns of newspapers outside of Russia, appear letters from Siberian exiles, detailing life there, and they are touching enough to harrow the soul ; but they have little effect upon the authorities. I am told that they would not object to the publication of these letters within the empire, as they take pride in keeping up the reputation of the country, since to reflect upon life in exile has a wholesome influence on would-be Nihilists.

CHAPTER XXI.

An interesting place to visit is the retail market at St. Petersburg. In the first place, the Russians eat the most strange things of any civilized people, and have the oddest way of displaying what they have to sell in the markets. Then they have a distinctive style of buying.

The building in which this market is conducted is low, long and broad. Here, as everywhere else, is found that staple article of food, caviar. As the season for vegetable and fruit-growing in Russia is so short, nearly all fruits and vegetables come from hot-houses. Grapes, peaches, pears and many kinds of berries come from Odessa and the Black Sea country. All are grown in hot-houses. Everything is sold by the pound, there being no measures on the Continent and few in England.

On every hand are strange-looking vegetables—artichokes that look like the flower of the thistle; cucumbers an inch in diameter, two feet long and green as grass; cabbages the size and shape of billiard balls; cranberries no larger than buckshot; pickled cauliflowers and pears having the appearance of sea lilies. The strawberries are as small as the blueberries; but the red raspberries are the largest and richest I ever saw. These are worth twenty copecks a pound.

In summer-time fish are all sold alive. It is rare that a dead fish is seen on the Russian markets, and then it is one of the large variety, like the salmon. Vats two or three feet deep, probably four feet square, and half-filled with water, swarm with fish; but each species is kept separate from the other, thus requiring many vats in a single stall, as there are numerous kinds of fish sold by every dealer. Long, slender, slimy eels, starlits, bass, pike, white bait, smelts and all the other varieties found in Russian waters may here be selected and taken away alive.

In the winter all fish except those which are dried or smoked are sold in a frozen state. During the early part of September fishermen begin to catch their winter supply and place them in vats. These are frozen in blocks to suit the orders of customers. The dealers buy many tons at a time; often enough to supply their demands for six months. The same is true of all kinds of meats. Beef, mutton, etc., are frozen at one time for the whole winter. Retail dealers lay in their supply of fresh meats for the entire winter during October; and the beef eaten in April next will be that which was slaughtered in October. This is on account of the extreme difficulty attending the killing of cattle in the winter and the expense of keeping them.

Salt sturgeon is for sale at every meat stall, and commands twenty-two copecks a pound. The serfs buy it, although no American could be forced to keep it on his stomach. The better grades of fish are more expensive by one-half than in America; and, in fact, all eatables are higher in Russia than in this country. Fish play an exceedingly important part in the domestic economy of the Russians. They are cooked in all conceivable styles, and not infrequently are eaten raw.

At Moscow the markets are conducted in an open square during the summer and in an old spacious building in winter. Here, as in St. Petersburg, there are runners for every stall, and as soon as a purchaser appears with a basket, he is besieged by the vendors. Men swarm around you with fowls, pieces of meat, fish and vegetable boxes, and, praising their goods, beg you to buy. Most of the dealers are unscrupulous and will take advantage by any hook or crook. The markets are open every day in the year, except Easter, when all business places are closed. Lamb's feet are among the choice tid-bits. The hoofs of calves are sold for soup-bones. The vegetables are watery and the fruits almost tasteless. Game and domestic fowls are all dressed, except for Jewish customers.

Everything in Russia is unique. The retail markets are no exception to the rule. They differ in every respect with those in other countries of Europe.

Probably the largest markets in Europe are at London. Here

there are permanent buildings and systems, as in New York, Boston,
Philadelphia and other American cities. The Covent Garden Market
afforded me a place for amusement and instruction one afternoon in
June. Southern France furnishes London the early fruits, and they
are received by consignment and sold at auction. It is common to
see a wagon-load of ox-heart cherries or peaches or plums knocked
off every minute to the highest bidder. The cries of the auctioneers
are almost deafening at times. The vegetables do not differ materially from those seen in American markets, except that tomatoes are
scarce, and corn and egg plants are never seen. The gardeners
seem to make a specialty of certain articles. One wagon will come
in from the garden loaded with only watercresses, while another has
mint, another garlic, another cucumbers, and so on; and each appears to avoid the possibility of a glut. Thus the prices are uniform.
The cherries are laid smoothly in neat, light, pine boxes, containing
one, two or three gallons; and those on top are as even as the teeth
in a saw. It is a scene worth looking at to witness the opening of
cases of onions, radishes, lettuce and other early vegetables at the
London markets, fresh from France; for there is the greatest neatness and order. Strawberries are grown in the vicinity of London to
an enormous size. The bulk of the meat comes from Australia and
America, the former shipping frozen and the latter live flesh. The
famous English mutton is bred in certain localities on a particular
feed, and even a patriotic Yankee must award it the palm of superi-
ority.

The markets at Vienna and Dresden are in open squares, and
protection from the sun and rain is afforded by umbrellas of heavy
white duck ten or twelve feet in diameter. At Dresden everything is
taken to market in long, slender carts drawn by dogs. The dogs are
large and sagacious, and know the location of their mistresses' stands
perfectly. As they approach the square in the early morning their
tongues protrude, they pant and froth at the mouth, and making a
bee-line for their destination, crawl under the carts and keep guard
until the day's work is done. Scarcely a man is seen about the market, either buying or selling.

Very similar are the markets at Hamburg, Germany. Here is a
low, long, one-story shed for the meat stalls, while the vegetables
and fruits are sold in the open square about. The meat is all hung
up on pegs; not a pound rests on a board. Fruits, vegetables, and
in fact almost everything, are sold from baskets and on the old-fash-

ioned scales. Garlic, great yellow cucumbers, carrots, sage, beans and herbs of every kind, are in profusion. Flowers and all sorts of notions are sold. Fish are cured in every conceivable form and are sold from baskets like vegetables.

Paris has her markets in the streets and sidewalks. On a Sunday morning one can scarcely get through certain portions of the city on account of the market fixings. Peas and beans are in boxes and baskets, and occupy a large portion of the space on every hand.

In Milan boys and little girls go around with small lambs, young pigeons and mocking-birds for sale. Macaroni is here a staple diet, as at Genoa and other Italian cities, and can be had at almost any price or in any shape.

The Campo de Fieorie Market at Rome is the most uncleanly of the lot. Women, men and children, in filth, flies and vermin, sell all kinds of noxious and unpalatable stuff, in dirty little rooms, and prefer to be unkempt rather than presentable on the same terms. In Rome during the warm weather, which is almost continuous, the laborers work from 4.30 a. m. till 12 noon; then rest till 3 and work till dark, which requires the markets to be open long hours. Boys push meat carts through the streets and dress lambs a fortnight of age on the front steps of a residence. Tripe, lemonade, fish, onions, honey, asparagus, the entrails of animals and fowls, pomegranates and citrons, are hauled around in the same carts and sold on the same scales.

The markets at Florence are conducted in the open air the year round, except for the sale of meats. These are in small shop-rooms, and the counters where the cutting is done are situated about ten feet above the floor. When you enter a Florentine meat-stall you are confronted by a man perched up like an auctioneer on a high counter.

The fish market at Venice is exceptionally interesting. It is located on the Grand Canal, in the heart of the city. As the gray of dawn appears scores of gondolas may be seen gliding in that direction. Each one drags a round willow or split basket, closely covered. These are filled with fish, each dealer making a specialty of a certain variety. The market is conducted under a long shed, and the baskets containing the fish remain in the water till a call is made by a customer. Then they are drawn up, the fish taken out, and down they are dropped till needed again. Early in the morning during the summer one can look from his window in any direction and see gondolas going toward the markets, filled with vegetables, women and children. The women are busy stringing beans, shelling peas or arranging the onions, carrots and other things in bunches. When they return at night the "merry song of the gondolier" may be heard if the day has been successful.

Berlin has the best market on the Continent : better buildings, greater supplies and superior goods. Fish are here sold from vats, and are kept alive. There is every variety of game and domestic fowl to be had within a thousand miles, and they are in the best condition. Steers, veal calves, lambs and other animals are dressed complete—that is, their heads and tails are skinned and kept intact on the trunks. Inflated bladders are hung about everywhere, for sale, while sausages, a dozen kinds of cheese, and mushrooms are to be had at every step. There is an abundance of fruit brought in by small row and canal-boats on the Spree every day, and everything is sold under the closest scrutiny of the market-masters.

CHAPTER XXII

HEY have a funny way of moving things in Moscow. I saw a procession of men going through the streets with the household effects of a well-known family. Four of them had the piano resting on their shoulders, while a range was carried by two others. Then followed men in single file with tables, mirrors, trunks, wash-boilers, tubs, bed-clothing and other goods on their heads. Wagons are seldom employed in hauling articles from one part of the city to another.

A Russian transfer or freight man carries around under his arm a head-pad about the size of the crown of a large cap. It is usually made of leather and stuffed with hair or hay. It is soft, and four inches thick. On a plate attached to his coat lapel is a word announcing that he is an expressman. He has no cart, horse or help. This man, single-handed and alone, contracts to remove all kinds of goods as rapidly and safely as if they were in charge of the great express companies of New York, Baltimore or Chicago. He associates with him, if there is heavy furniture or haste in the work, a number of his confreres ; and the men, sometimes to the aggregate of a score, simply walk into the house, pick up the goods, and carry them out and to their destination in a twinkle.

There is no groaning, packing, raising or adjusting about drays or wagons. When the men get their loads on their heads they start out, in Indian file, and make a little procession through the city. They never go down an unfrequented street, as they would lose an opportunity of advertising their trade. A Russian thinks no more of picking up a warm cooking-stove, placing it on his head and walking

a couple of versts, without rest, than an American would of carrying
an extra overcoat.

At Genoa, the principal port of Italy, I saw a moving scene a
few weeks before reaching Russia
which almost rivaled those I have
viewed in the Tsar's dominions.
A diminutive donkey was the vehicle of transfer. The dear little
thing was scarcely
larger than a six-
weeks-old calf, and
its ears were of
greater length and
breadth than those
of any ass I have
ever seen in the
United S t a t e s .

Across its back was a frame of
wood and straps quite as capacious as a hay-rack for a two-
horse wagon. The goods were
packed on in something like
this order : Center, dining-room
and writing tables ; a bookcase,
two stoves, three mattresses,
two trunks and four or five
satchels ; a refrigerator, a cabinet, half-a-dozen pictures in frames, a
mandolin, two accordions and a violin, two wardrobes, bed-clothing

and bedsteads for a large family, and the personal clothing and *bric-a-brac* of the entire household. On the head of the donkey were tied a bundle of newspapers, books and a roll of music, so that I had to stop and take a long, careful survey of the moving load before I could discover what furnished the motive power.

Immediately in the rear of this household-moving scene, which is the usual thing, came another donkey, which was used as a vehicle for retailing milk and fruits. On its back also was a large frame. On the frame were adjusted several heavy cans of milk, a dozen baskets of fruits, and the various measures and pair of scales used in the trade. Two minutes later I saw a train of a dozen donkeys loaded with iron for the improvement of the street railway. The iron was tied across the donkeys' backs the long way, and the weight would have been considered a good load for two horses in America. It is not uncommon to see a donkey carrying a load of railroad bars weighing two thousand pounds; and a ton is not a small wagon-load in most countries.

Speaking of railroad iron for the street tramways in Genoa, I must tell what kind of street railways they really have there, and in Russia also. I was on a street-car one morning in Genoa, going out toward the barracks. It was a single track, and no switches were in sight; yet I saw pretty soon another car coming on the same track and directly toward us. On it came, at a rapid run, till the two cars were within one hundred feet of each other. The movement was not slackened, and I began to fear there would be a collision, when the car I sat in suddenly turned off the track and went round the other. After bumping along a short distance on the boulders, it ran on the track again, never lessening its speed. I thought this a very strange and unusual movement, and began to conclude it was to avoid delay and to meet an emergency, when the car came to an abrupt corner of the street. Instead of keeping on the track, it ran off on the street and cut across, taking the track again when it was reached in the natural course of events.

There are no flanges on the wheels of the car, and therefore the streets and wheels are not injured in the least by the practice; yet the mules have a hard pull at it. But no one in Italy cares for mules or donkeys. On the contrary, the people rather enjoy seeing them have a hard time.

In St. Petersburg the street-cars are similarly constructed to those in Paris, but are a little larger. They are almost as long as a pas-

senger coach on an American railroad, have double decks, or two
stories, and accommodate over sixty passengers without crowding.
A stairway winds up at the rear of the cars leading to the long seats
above, over which is a wooden roof or canopy; and the passengers
have the privilege of a seat in the breeze above or in the inclosure
below, the latter being like the interior of American street-cars.
Eight horses are used when there is snow on the ground, four of them
being hitched abreast.

At Naples I saw a merchant moving his store. The goods appeared to be of a general character. A regular transfer wagon was
employed. This consisted of a vehicle with four wheels, sixteen
inches in diameter and of uniform size. To the wagon were hitched
a large Roman cow and a Naples donkey. The former was taller,
longer and more lank than any of the bovine family to be found in all
Texas, while the latter was as small as one of Barnum's Shetland po-
nies. The tongue of the vehicle was at the side of the cow, and the
donkey was hitched up on the other side of it. The idea I had at
first glance was that the donkey was thrown in as a kind of helper,
and that but little was expected of it. I soon saw my error. The
donkey was tied to or hitched against a whiffletree, while the cow
pulled from the side of the tongue. It can be seen that the draft of
the donkey was direct and effective, while that of the cow was indi-
rect and not effective. There were loads of hardware, casks of wine,
hogsheads of sugar and sacks of coffee, till the vehicle was a sight.

But the unfairness to and utility of the donkey were not yet.
When no more could be put on the wagon, which was only three feet
wide and twenty-five long, like a broad board, the donkey was loaded
up. First, three bags of coffee were tied on its back, and then a
bundle of pelts, as if the poor little thing would feel badly if it was
not employed as a beast of burden in all the ways one is used. No
one protested; no one seemed to pity the donkey. There were a
couple of old women who, while the load was being taken off, tried
to milk the cow. They were detected by the expressman's boy and
cuffed away from the premises. The cows are driven around the city
and milked as the fluid is sold.

One morning in Venice I was awakened from my slumbers by a
continuous yelling. There was a perfect din of voices below me, and
I got out of bed and went to the window, which overlooked one of
the usual thoroughfares—a narrow canal. Five gondolas were inter-
locked, and the gondoliers were cursing hot. Two or three times the

men took up their oars, and raising them aloft threatened to strike. I was not so much interested in the impending hostilities as the contents of the gondolas. These are longer, broader and deeper than the row-boats seen in the United States, and turn abruptly up at the bow, which is ornamented by a steel broad-ax. The propelling power is from the afterpart of the craft, and by a single long oar, which is twirled or worked in a socket against a post. Each gondola was filled with household goods. It looked as though three or four hotels were moving. Furniture, bed-clothing and personal effects of every description were piled up twenty feet high, so that it was impossible for a man in the stern to see where the prow of his gondola was going. Three of them were pointed in one direction, while two were bound for an opposite location. They had collided, and into the canal about six wagon-loads of goods were dumped. While the gondoliers were swearing and trying to extricate their gondolas, there were floating about in the water mattresses, tables and clothing ; and now and then a stove or a piece of tinware would drop off and go to the bottom of the canal. The perplexities of the men engaged seemed to be a little more wearing than those of the donkeys at Genoa and Naples, while the burdens appeared more irksome than those I saw on the heads of the less irritable Russians.

While going over the Alps of Switzerland I saw a household-moving scene which was quite as interesting and unique as any I have described. I was leaving Chamonix for Martigny, and had proceeded but a couple of miles, when, as we were winding up the side of a mountain five or six thousand feet high, I saw from the seat I occupied in the voiture what appeared to be a drove of pigs.

I watched the trailing objects for some minutes, when they disappeared, and I forgot them till two hours had elapsed, when my attention was suddenly attracted to seven old women, three old men and a boy, loaded with every conceivable personal effect used in a household. They were immediately ahead of our vehicle and in the middle of the road. Each had strapped on his or her back a basket of funnel shape, two feet across at the mouth, three feet long, and made of wood. These were filled with small articles ; after which bed-clothing, picture-frames, cases, cabinets and chairs were tied on the shoulders. One old woman had on her head and shoulders a small cooking-stove, while a man who looked to be four-score years old carried a big chest. Their journey was to be twenty-two miles that day, and the angle was an ascension of not less than fifteen degrees

on the average. I learned subsequently that nearly all the moving
done by the residents in the Alps is left to the old people—and they
grow to be centenarians, and so shriveled that the sex is distinguished
only by the garments they wear.   Nearly all the women have at their
throats great goitres—bags of serous fluid bigger than a hat.   Opinion is divided as to the causes which produce them.   The physicians
say they come from drinking glacier water, while those not versed in
medicine hold that they are the result of wearing straps about the
neck, suspended from which are baskets for the transportation of farm
products or express goods.

CHAPTER XXIII.

When finally I passed over the frontier of Russia and entered Germany, where there are free speech, a free press and free education, I found myself so impressed by what I considered imperiousness and oppression in the country of the Tsar, that I determined to make inquiry as to what had brought Russia into such unenviable prominence.

A short time afterward I was in London, where one hears more about the cruelties of Russia than in any other quarter of the globe. The Englishman hates Russia and her institutions quite as fervently as does the Russian despise the Englishman and his Government, forms and institutions. Before leaving America I read two or three books published by Sergius M. Stepniak, the widely-known Russian Nihilist, who has lived in exile for many years, but who from the outside manages to conduct one branch of the revolutionary movement in his country.

Having read so much attacking the Russian form of government by this man, and having seen a great deal of the country and its people, I resolved to meet him, learn how he lived, what character of man he is, his real objection to the empire he is fighting, how he is conducting his work, and what he has accomplished by it.

A Nihilist is always difficult to locate, and it is with more or less trouble that one can induce him to talk. Stepniak is a well-known character in London. He is thirty-eight years old, large, finely-developed, intellectual and cultured. His home is in the midst of a beautiful grove in St. John's Wood a suburb of the world's metropolis. It is a charming spot where his modest little cottage is located, and I found the great Nihilist to be in most respects like the average *littcratcur*, with an abundance of books, magazines and newspapers about him, and a fund of mental food for the entertainment of his guests. In an afternoon's talk with him, and after reading all of the books he has written, I am enabled to present the Nihilistic side of the Russian struggle, and that which here follows may be regarded as the presentation by Mr. Stepniak of his view of the question.

Nihilism is revolution. Nihilism is also Communism and So-
cialism. But Nihilism, as the word is generally used by the revolutionists, does not necessarily imply violence. It means concentrated,
systematic effort to supplant the existing forms of government and
law with other forms and laws.

The most intelligent Communists or revolutionists believe in
a constitutional form of government. They recognize, however,
that a Republic, or representative government, cannot be instituted
and maintained successfully without education. They are therefore
striving first for public free schools. They want regularly-constructed
statutory and constitutional laws, so that there may be system in
public as well as private affairs. After the people are educated, then
will come the proposition to change the present form of government.
Under the existing ignorance, illiteracy and superstition it is acknowl-
edged by the revolutionists themselves that a constitutional form of
government, or, in fact, any change of government, would be imprac-
ticable. The people, after education, want free thought as to religion
and the disestablishment of the Church of Russia—in fact, such religious freedom as Garibaldi gave Italy. They want free speech and
a free press, so that the various propositions for changes in the ruling
of the country may be discussed and the most advisable plan adopted.

All of these demands having been rejected at the very outset by
the Tsar, and an effort made to put a check upon the growing clamor
for education and a free expression of sentiment, there is left but one
recourse, and that is revolution—a resort to force for the purpose of
bringing about what civilization naturally develops. At present there
is no such thing as the right of petition. The Tsar and his Council
refuse to hear expressions from the people on the proposition of education, or any change in the form of government. The revolutionists
hope to force the Tsar and his counselors to change their present attitude by presenting, in an impassioned way, a consensus of public
opinion, showing that their demands are not those of any clique or
organization, but those of the masses. If the objects desired are not
attained by persuasive and argumentative means then revolution,
or war, is to be resorted to.

Russians are proverbially lovers of their country. It is not a
mere dislike to things natural that has led to extreme measures to
change the condition of affairs, but the constant growth of imperiousness on the part of the Tsar in the first instance, and the spreading
overbearance of the aristocracy latterly. The revolutionists claim to

be in a defensive position. They are oppressed beyond endurance, and justify the use of violence as the only means of throwing off the yoke which has sent one-third of the present generation into base servitude and threatens the generations to come. Unlike the revolutionists in Ireland, Spain and some other countries, where there are governmental disturbances, the Russian Nihilists have made no effort to spread their work outside their own domain, and have not solicited sympathy from foreigners.

No one should be condemned without first having been heard in his own defense. The present systems of general and local government make this absolutely impossible, owing to the Tsar's despotism and the autocratic bureaucracy surrounding him. The active body of Nihilistic conspirators comprises simply Radicals, Land Nationalists and Social Democrats. Each of these expect various fruits from the establishment of a national representation, just as the various sections of the Irish Home Rulers do ; but it is conceded that this cannot be a matter of consideration at present, since there is a vast difference between the condition of the people in Ireland and in Russia. The Irish are educated and the Russians are illiterate.

Most of the work of the revolutionists is now being conducted by the clandestine publication of papers and pamphlets propagating the idea of liberty and calling Russians to a sense of their dignity as men and citizens. These teachings are penetrating the ranks of the army and navy, and are touching the judgment of officials. The revolutionists take more encouragement from this fact than any other. They believe that in the event of an outbreak at any time there will be a general disintegration of the organized forces of the empire ; and that when it comes to war the majority will be on the side of those striving for liberty. They do not acknowledge that they are rebelling against the individual rulers of the country, but contend that it is rebellion against despotism—the excessive power of the Tsar. The conspirators admit that they believe the assassination of a Tsar, occasionally, is essential to the success of their movement, and that it is commendable at any time, on the ground that it impresses the rulers and those about them with the deep earnestness and determination of the people who protest against existing conditions.

By the interpretation of the vague laws of the country the revolutionists and the sympathizers with assassins are equally guilty of the high crime of assassination of the Tsar, and are equally punished. Even the readers of the regicidal papers who have not immediately turned informers are, according to the strict terms of the Russian laws, accessories to regicide. They are punished by death whenever the Government chooses to apply the full rigor of the law. This extreme interpretation of the law covering conspiracy against the crown is made for the purpose of obliterating the propagation of public sentiment antagonistic to the present form of government.

It is held by the Tsar that even the slightest dissatisfaction with the *status quo* should be exterminated; and if necessary the person directly affected should be destroyed with the principle he advocates. The revolutionists do not defend the principle of political assassination except in extreme instances. They hold that assassination is the last defense within their power, and that when they are driven at bay this may be resorted to with justification.

For the purpose of ascertaining just what the natives at large thought of the laws and powers of the Tsar there have been, during the past decade or two, a few trials by jury of persons attempting the life of the Tsar or those of his immediate Council. In January, 1878, Vera Zassulibet, a young Nihilist girl, shot at the chief of the St. Petersburg police, General Trepoff, inflicting on him a wound in the abdomen, which for many weeks held his life in suspense. By special order she was tried by a jury, for the purpose of arriving as nearly as possible at the conclusion the public held in the case. The girl was promptly acquitted on trial in the March following.

This and similar isolated instances are constantly pointed out by the revolutionists to show that public sentiment condemns the present system of trial without jury. Common law-breakers are sometimes tried by jury, though the privilege has never been extended to political offenders, who are tried by special courts, or rather special commissions, nominated by the Government *ad hoc*.

It is held that the Russian autocracy has used to the utmost the advantage which the commissions afford and enormous military forces give it to suppress the legitimate aspirations of the people, and to retain a regime hateful to all of the educated classes, disastrous to their material and moral welfare and perilous to the future of the nation and the state.

During the last fifteen years of reaction the press has been gradually crushed, because it did not cease to speak of the popular grievances. In the absence of representative institutions the press was the only vehicle to give utterance to the popular needs. Now Russia has practically no press at all. The censorship and the private orders of the ministers prevent it from speaking upon any questions of public importance. ˙Thus, to quote one illustration out of thousands, while all the European papers are indignant at the barbarous suppression by the Cossacks' whips and the butt-end of soldiers' guns of the purely scholarly disturbances in the Russian universities and the killing of several disarmed students, the Russian papers are not allowed to say anything, to publish any detail, beyond the mere reprint of the official announcement of the closing of such and such university.

The popular education, upon which the future of the nation reposes, has been subjected, since 1874, to restrictions which became more and more tyrannical as the reaction increased, because the Government realizes that the masses, in becoming educated, will see where the cause of their suffering lies, and will cease to be obedient. The inviolability of the person, all the judicial guarantees, the freedom of speech, or rather the freedom of talk, in the sacred precincts of men's own houses, are trampled upon shamelessly, because they constitute a standing danger to the despotism. For words uttered at private parties, in private houses, people of all ages, classes and both sexes are arrested, kept in prison, *durante beneplacito*, or exiled to Siberia and other desolate regions by hundreds and thousands, without even the formality of trial. A simple order of the police suffices. No counsel is allowed to visit them ; they are kept ignorant of the name of their accuser ; they are informed but vaguely of the nature of the charge brought against them. Very often they are not told of what they are accused, and have to start on their melancholy journey with nothing but the knowledge that the police conceived suspicions that their political faith was unsound.

The men and women engaged in the revolutionary movement are generally of very good character. They are with scarcely an exception educated. They have become feverish from the goadings of imperiousness, and are simply striving to obtain freedom. They hold that their cause is spreading ; that they already have a majority of the populace with them, and that it is only a question of time when they will obtain what they are striving for, even should it be necessary to secure it by bloodshed.

"Liberty won by assassination !" exclaimed the renowned Nihilist. "The phrase has an ugly sound. We are the first to acknowledge it and to regret it. But is the idea altogether new ? Liberty snatched from the oppressions of all the dark ages was the result of

struggle, strife and bloodshed. Why, then, should not the assassination of Alexander II. prove useful? It is not the apology for terror-
ism that we are making, but the analysis of it. The anomaly presented by the struggle for liberty in Russia is but a reflection of the
anomalies inherent in the social condition of the country. In other
countries which have had a genuine national culture liberal ideas
have been developed concurrently with the material and intellectual
development of the classes that stand in need of them, and the result
has been the overthrow of the autocracy by the revolutionary movement; the bourgeoisie, valuing itself upon its influence with the
working class, and especially with the more intelligent and excitable
operatives of the towns, has stirred up the people to overthrow the
ancien regime, and establish upon its ruins the parliamentary institutions that belong to the new political order. But in Russia nothing
of this sort is possible. The whole nation languishes under its barbarous and incapable government, and the agricultural class suffers
most of all. Political freedom will be of the utmost benefit to the
peasants by enabling them to realize the agrarian reforms which they
foolishly expect to be made by the Tsar. But this they do not understand. And the class which has to strive for political freedom is that
to which it is a boon and necessity in itself—the educated class, called
in Russia the intelligent class. It has no distinctive origin or position except such as comes by professional occupation. It includes
the nobility and the educated part of the bourgeoisie, sons of the
church, as well as officers of the Government. It is upon this class,
nourished from childhood on the liberal thoughts of the best European thinkers, and permeated by the most advanced democratic ideas,
that the actual despotism presses most painfully. Rebellion under
the existing condition of affairs is inevitable, and we have it now in
fact. Turn Nature out the door and she comes back through the
window.

"It cannot be denied that foreigners, provided they are sufficiently well informed, are the best judges of a country. They possess,
in the first place, the most valuable requisite for dispassionate observation. Besides, as they are new to the country, their senses and
intellects are more keenly alive to peculiarities that pass unnoticed by
those born and educated in it. At the time of some great crisis in
the history of a nation it is often given to foreigners to discover the
first symptoms of coming events. Thus the revolutionists point to
this fact with pride, in connection with their claim that all foreigners

interesting to study the position taken by native Russians who are loyal to their ruler in advocating his cause. I formed an acquaintance with one of the most intelligent and instructive of the Tsar's late subjects upon my return from Russia to Washington. Count Charles d'Arnaud was born, educated, and spent the major part of his life in Russia. He is a member of one of the best-known families of the empire. He was in the Russian engineer corps during the Crimean war, and was one of the army which resisted the gallant charge of Tennyson's Noble Six Hundred at the Battle of Balaklava. During the American civil war he came to this country, was commissioned as a Captain, and assigned to duty on General Rosecrans' staff. His engineering knowledge and ability as a topographer proved to be invaluable to the Union forces. General Grant ascribed to him great credit for the manner in which he, at extreme personal risk, prepared a rough map of the surroundings of Shiloh, to which was due in part the success of the Union army at Hornets' Nest.

In talking with Count d'Arnaud about Russia and her institutions he gave me the following outline of the position of those who uphold the existing form of government:

"Much of the information obtained by journalists, travelers and casual students while in Russia is wholly misleading. Failing to understand the language, habits and peculiarities of the natives, they obtain their facts from sojourners who have no sympathy with or interest in the country; from foreigners who have taken up their residence there and are as unappreciative and prejudiced as themselves; from the few natives known to the world as Nihilists, who get their inspiration from Bakounin, Krapotkine and other disciples, and from still other sources which are more insidious in their methods and successful in their aims to array the English-speaking peoples of the world against Russia by constantly crying oppression and despotism. I refer to England, English diplomacy and the English press. They are evidently moved by jealousy of the growing power and approaching supremacy of Russia in the political affairs of the Old World.

"The United States has been my home for over thirty years; I am an ardent admirer of its constitution and laws, and I did my share toward keeping the States united by service in the war of the rebellion. Yet with all my love of the liberty inculcated into me by this experience I fail to see any necessity for a change in the form of the Russian government. It is thoroughly adapted to the wants of the

people.   Under it they have attained a high degree of civilization,
power and prosperity.   Both the Government and people hold the
United States in high esteem, so that it is not unreasonable to ask
that Americans do not hastily judge them by the vaporings of their
enemies, who, though actuated by different motives, all aim to injure
Russia in the estimation of travelers by appeals to sentiment merely, in
which the Tsar is pictured as a savage despot, who delights in torturing
his subjects, and has no care or concern for their welfare.   I have known
the present Tsar—Alexander III.—almost since his infancy, and can
assure you that he is one of the most accomplished, liberal and en-
lightened monarchs that ever sat upon a throne ; a monarch who constantly studies the welfare of his people ; a monarch who is mild-
mannered, gentle and kind, and who continualy strives to ascertain
the needs of his subjects, and even now stands ready to adopt whatever system of government would be most conducive to the welfare
of Russia.   For these qualities he is almost worshiped by the people,
all reports to the contrary notwithstanding.

"Russia is much larger in area than the United States, and has a
population of nearly one hundred millions, made up of a great many
different races and tribes, speaking as many languages, differing in
habits, religion and modes of life, and in many cases having been
enemies long ago.   Any one acquainted with the history of its rapid
rise and progress will readily acknowledge that the Romanoff dynasty
has built substantially and solidly with disorganized and discordant
material, carrying the people forward from the primitive to their
condition to-day.   And all this has been accomplished under the
present form of government.   Yet the Nihilistic cry, which seems to
be most effective now and upon which they endeavor to justify their
dastardly attempts upon the life of the Emperor, is his refusal to establish a constitutional government.   Americans may look upon such
a demand as most reasonable ; but if they understand the situation
and look at it from the standpoint of a patriotic Russian they will
readily see their mistake.

"There is no demand among the great mass of the Russian people
for such a change.   Suppose a constitutional government had been
established before the liberation of the serfs.   Could the much-la-
mented Alexander II., with a stroke of his pen, have been able to
free twenty-six millions of them ?   When we recall how much blood
and treasure were expended to secure the freedom of only four millions of people in the United States, we can form some idea of what

the undertaking would have been in Russia. Then, instead of only a South, like we had, slavery extended over the whole empire, and the Parliament would have been fully controlled by the slave-owners. The aristocracy and landed proprietors would have been masters of the situation without fear of interference, and they would have taken care not to allow their slaves to be freed. This great act of the so-called despotic Government of Russia ought to outweigh nearly all the charges, true and untrue, made by its enemies.

" But there are several other unassailable objections to a Russian Parliament.

"Such a body, which must include representatives of all the classes, creeds and nationalities, would be a Babel of confusion and a Bedlam of conflicting interests. Imagine a parliamentary body composed of Poles, Germans, Cossacks, Tartars, Mohammedans, Greek Catholics, Roman Catholics, Turkomans, Jews, Copts, and scores of other wholly dissimilar races and nationalities, bitterly opposed, antagonistic to each other. Could such a body legislate for a great empire like Russia? Would the same legislation answer for the Tartar and the Pole, for the Mohammedan and the Roman Catholic? I believe not; and I am confident that constitutional government is not wanted in Russia except by a few idle dreamers and enthusiasts.

" It will require very many years to educate the Russians up to the proper appreciation of constitutional government, even at the rapid rate of progress made under the Romanoff dynasty. And until this education is accomplished centralization of power is in the hands of the Tsar and his counselors ; and the judicious exercise of the same is the only governmental system capable of saving Russia from dismemberment and disruption. The division of the empire into provinces ruled directly by a Governor appointed by the Tsar and a Council selected from among the people thereof amounts to practical local self-government ; and the erection of each of the many distinct nationalities into separate provinces removes all the danger of a clashing of interests such as would be sure to result from any imperial parliamentary system. Another and by no means a lesser advantage to be derived from this system is the gradual and healthy assimilation which is going steadily forward, and which will surely result in breaking the tribal and racial barriers now operating to the disadvantage of the country.

" The criminal law of Russia, of which we hear so much unfavorable and unjust criticism, is nothing more than the code of Napoleon, with a few minor changes. The charge that the administration of the criminal law is harsh and tyrannical is a libel on the judiciary of the empire, which has been the first of the great nations to abolish the death penalty. There is no capital punishment in Russia, except in aggravated cases of high treason, such as attempts on the life of the Tsar. But the impartiality with which the law is enforced is proverbial. Prince and peasant are equally punished for equal offenses; and the rigor with which the former are handled for transgressions against the law is a matter of history.

"We are told in glowing language that free speech and a free press are myths in Russia; but we are seldom told the true reason why. We are not told that among an excitable and warlike people, such as are many of the Russians who retain much of their old turbulent spirit, the free press and free speech of demagogues and anarchists would produce chaos and bloody revolution, in which there would be no safety for life or property. Even in free America there is a limit to free speech and a free press, as was shown in the conviction and execution of the Anarchists in Chicago and the imprisonment of Herr Most in the city of New York. The aim of the Russian Government is to curb this element; and it goes without saying it is justified in taking an hundredfold more vigorous measures than are taken in America. Generally the seed of demagogy falls by the wayside or is dropped upon rocks in this Republic, where it withers and dies; but in Russia it finds far more congenial climate and fruitful soil.

"I insist that the Russian system of banishment to Siberia is far more humane than the English method of disposing of political prisoners. How many Irishmen have languished and died, or were broken in health and spirit in English prison dungeons! and yet we heard no great outcry against England. The situation in Russia to-day is certainly preferable to that created by English coercion in Ireland.

"The passport system, which is said to be so obnoxious to American and European merchants and tourists, is really an absolute necessity as an agency for the suppression of crime. The police and detective systems have not attained anything like the perfection enjoyed in America and elsewhere, while the demand for them is much greater. The wonderful skill by which the names and careers of criminals are all recorded and their movements watched is almost unknown in Russia. Every town and hamlet is not connected with its neighbors and with the great cities by electric currents, as is the case here. By the systematic use of all these advantages America and other equally favored nations are enabled to maintain law and order and the security of life and property without resort to the repressive measures needed in Russia. The best substitute for these advantages is the passport system ; and it is not only a necessity, but is demanded by the educated and law-abiding people of the empire as a means of self-preservation. Under its operation a thief or law-breaker of any description, or a band of them, cannot commit crime with impunity in one locality and then emigrate to another. Before getting the necessary passport the antecedents of every applicant are ascertained ; and the good are distinguished from the bad and treated accordingly. Very naturally the law-breakers and agitators regard this as a hardship; but their fellow-citizens demand it as a safeguard against the machinations of both. The fee charged for the passport is made necessary by the system, which is expensive. It is justly regarded as one of the sources of revenue.

"True, there is no compulsory education in Russia, and no adequate provision is made for the education of the masses; but the facilities afforded are fully as good as could be expected under the circumstances. Russia is a new nation, comparatively speaking. She is not up to the age in educational matters, but is constantly striving to that end ; and even now every young man, be he rich or poor, can be educated at the public expense by making application to the local representative of the Government, according to custom. Free education is but a new departure. It originated in the West, and is moving eastward. We know that for many years after the American war of the rebellion the educational system of the Southern States was deplorably defective and inadequate; and even at this day some of the States make but feeble attempts to provide free education. Of course the liberation of the slaves was the reason. Therefore, before criticising the Russian educational system, it is but fair to recall the fact that she is dealing with twenty-six millions of recently-liberated serfs.

"The utter ludicrousness of Stepniak's attempt to pose as the spokesman of the Russian people needs just a passing comment. Bakounin and Krapotkine, the originators of Anarchism and Nihilism, whose disciple he is, were banished from the Swiss Republic, and Krapotkine was imprisoned in France for advocating the form of government they desire in Russia. Then the theories and doctrines which Stepniak would promulgate have been condemned by the tribunals of both the Republics last named, as dangerous to society and the security of life and property."

THE END.